Metaphorosis

November 2018

Beautifully made speculative fiction

Also from Metaphorosis Books

Reading 5X5: Readers' Edition
Reading 5X5: Writers' Edition

Best Vegan Science Fiction & Fantasy

Best Vegan SFF of 2017
Best Vegan SFF of 2016

Metaphorosis Magazine

Metaphorosis: Best of 2017
Metaphorosis: Best of 2016
Metaphorosis 2017: The Complete stories
Metaphorosis 2016: Nearly Complete Stories
Monthly issues

by B. Morris Allen

Susurrus
Allenthology: Volume I
Tocsin: and other stories
Start with Stones: collected stories
Metaphorosis: a collection of stories

Metaphorosis

November 2018

edited by
B. Morris Allen

Metaphorosis Books

Neskowin

ISSN: 2573-136X (online)
ISBN: 978-1-64076-120-9 (e-book)
ISBN: 978-1-64076-121-6 (paperback)

November 2018

The Little G-d of Łódź

Evan Marcroft

On September 6, 1939, a Rabbi and Kabbalist named Yitzchok Falk sets fire to the Great Synagogue of Łódź. "The Germans will burn it anyway," he tells his apprentice they drag a body out of the trunk of his car. "Let it burn without victims, and for a good reason." The boy, Max, who holds the feet, only nods.

They carry the body in and lay it out in the prayer hall. It is a young man near Max's thirteen years and fifty seven kilos, dressed in his clothes. He died of a broken neck, not of their doing, and was obtained at great cost. From his coat the rabbi produces a rag-corked bottle and a heavy black key, the latter of which he presses into his apprentice's hand. "Everything is yours now," he tells the boy. "Do with it what you will, if you will good. But your life has become a precious resource. Keep it from those who want it and give it to those who need it." His voice breaks under the weight of emotion. "Do not loathe those who loathe you. Just live, Max. We are Jews; we know dark times will pass."

Max buries the key in his fist, but only nods.

He stays long enough to help his adopted father start the fire, touching flame to the parched books in the study hall, dousing the holy ark in petrol. He finds that a Torah scroll smolders with the same smell as any other paper. He escapes as the flames begin to creep towards the rafters, leaving his master to his last act of charity. The gunshot is a raindrop amidst a downpour.

Max flies through cobbled streets until it is safe to stop and catch his breath. Only then does he crumple up and discard his master's final words. There is no room left in his heart for them, for with apologies it is already so full of bile and venom and *hate.*

The key opens the hidden lock of a secret room in his master's house. There, where by lamplight Rabbi Falk taught him of the sefirot and the boustrophedontic Folded Name of G-d, are kept many tomes of ancient Tradition. The *Sodei Razayya*, the *Sefer Yetzirah*, and others more arcane still, illuminated ledgers of demons and angels, books of power, all disguised cleverly in the bindings of Christian bibles. Max takes them all.

The Germans will roll over this place in a matter of days and pave everything, stone and knowledge alike, into a road going east. Same as the synagogue, which would have burned tomorrow if not today. In boot tread and tank tread they will track all that is *jude* across Poland until there is only dust left of it.

But Max knows well there is power in dust.

Seven months later, in the spring of 1940, Max has a new family. The rabbi, ever prescient, made the arrangements for him well before he falsified Max's death. He has a new name; rest in peace, Max Steinberg, and welcome back from abroad cousin Oskar Kac. His aunt and uncle are Monica and Dieter, his little blonde cousin Else, and they live together in a modest house in the Sródmiescie district. They are ethnic German—happily registered *Volksdeutsche*—and they are Christians. Max could not ask for a better place to hide.

It is easy to be Oskar the Christian. In some ways it is an easier life than Max the *judenschwein*. The facets of the faith are not so different from his own. A crucifix is not the worst thing that can be tied around one's neck. His false family are Jewish sympathizers, educated people, and they are very kind to him. They have made sure he is comfortable in their cellar and allow him to eat supper with them. Little Else in particular is a blessing. She is a dim but charming girl who is happy to help Max fill the empty hours when it is too risky to be outside.

And yes, his features are Aryan enough that he can even walk about in broad daylight, so long as he carries his forged papers like he would clutch shut an open wound.

Max may walk free, but he has not escaped the ghetto. Is he supposed to not hear it when the Orpo executes men and women in the streets, or smell the bodies strung up until they rot free of the rope? That pigpen between Inflancka and Drewnoska Street is where his kind is deemed to belong, and at all times he feels its subtle gravity threatening to draw him in if he is not absolutely vigilant.

Yet he is there, watching from the crowd, as the wall is put up around the ghetto. The barrier is a flimsy thing, green wood garnished with barbed wire. The weight of all the bodies behind it would easily bowl it over. And why don't they? There must be thousands of them cramped into a tenth as many rooms turned cells. A universe of yellow stars. The few Germans who strut to and fro outside the fence would be drowned in them.

But those hot, fresh first days where anything could still have happened mature into weeks. More Jews are shipped in from outside the city and poured into the ghetto. What keeps it from rupturing like a full bladder, Max does not know—the Germans are geniuses in the science of cruelty. And still, he watches its occupants shuffle a little closer together, tromping in their own overflowing feces, making room.

They do not fear the *Nazis*, he has come to believe.

Not as much as they fear their sharp-edged *eye*. The eye that flutters from every storefront, that lolls from every shattered window. Bloodshot, lidless, its pupil a black windmill slashed into a cataracted iris, glowering over all. When the Orpo is gone, the eye observes. They call it the *Hakenkreuz*, though Max knows of many other names. The symbol came from somewhere in the Orient. India perhaps. It had meant only good things once, to many peoples, but the Germans can corrupt even the intangible, bend good to the work of evil.

In their hands it has become a lens for something to peer balefully through. Something that loathes the Jew and gluts on their suffering. Max knows not what name to call the entity. But whenever its indentured eye meets his, Max refuses to look away. Does the thing behind the *swastika* see the truth of him? Let it. Those trapped in the ghetto may be powerless before it, but he is not.

He has dirt, and a word.

In the cellar of the Kac house, Max is making a golem.

For the last several months he has scavenged and saved to purchase its components: Lengths of stiff wire, for structure; basic sculpting tools; eighty kilograms of clay in blocks. Concealing it all from the Kacs was a chore. Sculpting it by hand, by himself, in a night, is even harder.

Max misses the old rabbi sorely. This task is too much for just him. His hands know the way, but his father's had been there and back. Max is only fourteen. Too young to be alone.

Still, grueling hours transform the mound of wet clay into an approximation of the human form. Its eyes are featureless bulbs, its mouth a gash. No nose or ears. His creation is smaller than he anticipated it would be; nearly two and a half meters tall but thin as a skeleton, its skull an oblong club. Max would have preferred to whittle it mighty and broad from the riverbank as Rabbi Loew did, but the curfew made that so dangerous as to be impossible. Its strength will have little to do with such trivia as mass and proportion.

Max stands over his work and sponges the sweat from his neck and brow. *My Adam*, he thinks, with pride. For was mankind not born through a similar art, cut out of the stuff of the earth?

For an hour Max circles his creation, whispering a string of names that scorch his tongue to pronounce, draping the golem in veils of meaning. Next he draws purified water from an urn and ladles it up and down the golem's chest. Wherever it trickles, the clay takes on the oily sheen of living skin. He strikes a match, holds it to the golem's feet until its soles are chapped and cracked as an old man's. Lastly, Max crouches over the golem and breathes into its dent of a mouth. His heart accelerates as its chest rises atop imaginary lungs.

Earth, water, fire, and air. There is only one thing left.

There is one thing Max did not prepare in advance, lest it slip into irreverent hands. On a slip of torn paper no larger than his thumb, he writes a shem—a Name of G-d.

He folds it in two, gigs it with a pin, and tacks it to the floor of the golem's mouth.

Eyes of solid clay snap open.

Max retreats into the corner as the golem climbs onto its feet. The hump of its scalp scrapes against the floorboards overhead. Overlarge hands swing limply at its sides. It is a mottled thing; red clay in places, ruddy flesh in others. Fingernails have sprouted on one hand, but the tip of its phallus has already broken off. It is imperfect, yes. And glorious as salvation always is.

Max would cry out, if it would not wake his family.

"Can you speak?" Max asks in Hebrew.

The golem shakes its head.

"Do you have knowledge?"

The golem nods.

"I have created you. Will you serve me?"

The golem nods again.

Max unfolds a photograph from his trouser pocket. "This man is *Hauptmann* Rudolf Pancke. He is an evil man: he has murdered many children of Israel for no crime. He profits from the theft of their possessions. Kill him, tonight, wherever he is."

The golem nods a third time. It does not look at the photograph.

"Men will try to stop you," Max adds. "If they are not Jews, kill them as well. When you are finished, do not return here—destroy yourself, or at least the shem in your mouth. Do you understand?"

The golem is already leaving.

The following morning Max swallows his exhaustion and requests to accompany the Kacs on their shopping. While Else is fitted for a new church dress and Mrs. Kac collects the week's groceries, Max cocks an ear to the gossip running wild up and down Piotrkowska Street.

Not four hours past, Rudolf Pancke was discovered murdered in his home, his throat crumpled as though by a vice, face black with trapped blood. His wife Gertrude was dead as well, her forehead flattened against their stovetop. Whoever attacked them tore their door of its hinges and took five bullets from Pancke's sidearm without leaving a drop of blood.

Max had been expecting to feel happy. Vindicated.

Instead, he feels hungry

A Jew must be the culprit of course. A rare brute of higher cunning than his breed, escaped from the ghetto with slaughter on the mind. Or perhaps one who had evaded being swept up with the rest of them, for despite assurances, there are surely many still skulking under floorboards like rats. Over the following days, Max watches the Orpo presence around the ghetto increase dramatically, In a show of force, they drag ten young men from their homes and execute them on the blackened steps of what had been the old Stara Synagogue. Those deaths are his fault as well. Max accepts that and moves on. They were dead long before he killed them.

With every new invader he sees on the street corner, he feels more powerful. They are war now, because of *him*. *Their* lives are in *his* hands.

But the same time, each reminds Max of just how many Germans there are in Łódź. Months of caution and preparation, a bucket of sweat, for only one head. Two, if he counts the wife.

He wants more. But how to begin? Where does one bite first to devour a mountain? This problem keeps him awake through humid nights. Max is starving with too much on his plate, from the patrolling officers who inflict a thousand little brutalities along their route, to that quisling Rumkowski who runs the ghetto in the German's stead. Who would be worth the time and risk, the blind retaliation? Of course he could simply knock down the walls of the ghetto, but that would hardly be productive. Animals escaped from the zoo are most often just shot.

Although he frets, he does not fear, for he knows his cause is just. In the darkened sky above the ghetto he has beheld the archangel Metatron, the right hand of G-d, with an aureole of flaming eyes about his brow and wings of gold forty thousand cubits in span. None but Max can see him—no, they merely duck under awnings and complain of the rain. Oh, if only the prisoners there could feel the hem of his alabaster robe pooled about their feet, they would know hope, for he who led the Israelites from Egypt has now come to Łódź. In one hand he holds a sword of smithied lightning, crackling and spitting; the other is pointed down in scorn at the ghetto administration headquarters.

The heavenly scribe speaks not a word, but its message is evident.

It is Else, of all people, who provides Max the breakthrough he needs. She has a little cloth doll named Odie, whom she carries with her everywhere. While playing one afternoon, a thread in Odie's leg catches on a jutting nail and tears beyond repair. She is distraught, until her mother sews the doll a new leg from an old paisley headscarf. Else sees happy enough with the result, not minding the incongruous limbs. The doll is still a doll. One material is as good as another.

How far might that principle travel before it broke down?

Golems have historically been exclusively from clay, for two reasons. The first is practicality: they have to be wrought from earth, and clay is easy to shape. The second is tradition; it has been done that way since the time of the rabbi Rava. But Max suspects now that this way of thinking has stunted the possibility of the golem. It is the twentieth century now; the world is wider and vastly deeper than it was.

Rabbi Falk taught him more than the Kabbalah in the years they'd had together. Max was better with letters and numbers than most his age, though his aptitudes were science and history. For instance, he knew that some thirty-five years ago a German Jew named Einstein proved the ancient theory that all creation is composed of invisibly small particles—particles that logically can then be rearranged to construct whatever one likes. It seemed to Max that if one were to examine any two items on a small enough scale, they would essentially be the same amalgamation of substances.

In that realm where atoms are the size of planets, everything is dirt.

Through the summer and autumn of 1940, Max sets out to make golems from everything.

Very quickly he proves his theory true. A man made of branches and twine takes little time and less artistic finesse than clay, and, as he discovers, animates nearly as well. When imbued with a name of G-d, a brace of twigs will crack and twist into a hand of five functional fingers. Knots will blink and suddenly be eyes, and hoary bark will sprout goosebumps in the cold. And most importantly, though at its thickest it may be no bigger around than his calf, it will possess the strength to crumble a brick in one fist.

With this first success to whet his appetite, Max attacks the subject with renewed fervor. He finds that it is easier to smuggle other materials into his room than clay, especially via the cellar's small window overlooking a strip of weeds beside the house.

From the moment the Kacs go to bed, Max toils at innovating the concept of the golem. Wood works well, as does sacking, and especially metal. Over the course of two sweltering nights in late August he patches together a child-sized thing of scrap pilfered from a garbage heap near the factory where the Germans have put the Jews to work. Although its gait is ungainly, its pipe neck inflexible, it handily eviscerates an Orpo captain with fingers of serrated steel, leaving him to be found in an alley the next morning.

That is good; two nights is not. Max can do better.

He finds efficiency in hybridism. Clay is ideal flesh, but sticks will function as limbs, and anything will serve for a head. With each golem the time and energy needed to acquire its pieces shrinks. What helps, Max finds, is to inscribe the shem directly on the skin of the golem, as not every one can have a mouth. It seems to provide them with a shade more humanity —broader swathes of flesh, more articulate digits—than his previous method.

Some turn out laughable, jiggumbob men with old kettles for heads, clopping about on wooden clogs. But function supersedes aesthetics. Broom-handle legs, knives for fingers, rags stuffed with rags for feet—all perfectly lethal. Night after night he sends them out with a name and a mission, infesting the shadows of Łódź with scuttling, clanking deaths wrought of its own matter. Max feels unfettered, a renegade genius in his field. What *else* had others not dared to attempt? He wonders how *small* a golem could be, how sneaking and insidious. Could a shem be written with a needle? A hair?

He wonders how *immense* as well.

He wonders that often.

Not every golem is successful. Some are destroyed by happenstance; an incidental scratch can obliterate a shem. And it was inevitable that one would be caught in the act or fail by some unforeseeable chance. On the night of October 12th, a Gestapo officer bursts into his headquarters with an arm lacerated in a thousand places, gabbling about shear-handed scarecrows. They public thinks him mad, but a month later, a boneless poppet made of a straw-stuffed Polish uniform is speared in the headlights of a truck full of German soldiers. A hail of gunfire blasts it to tatters, but whispers of it spread like fleas off a rat.

Golem. Max begins to hear the word from other lips.

Else asks what it means one evening as the family takes its supper. Max must feign disinterest. A golem, Mister Kac explains, in that tone fathers use to shrink adult concepts into child ones, is a big man made from clay and a magic word. It is a way for powerless people to become powerful. The legend goes that a Jewish holy man in a city called Prague created one to protect his people from their enemies. But although the golem was strong and fearless, it one day went mad and became a danger to everyone. So remember, Else, that sometimes the answer is worse than the problem.

Over the course of weeks, the Germans clamp tight about the city. They begin to move in larger groups. They publically scoff at the notion of a clay man murdering by night, but the streets start to empty themselves a little earlier come nightfall. Perhaps they, of all people, believe in some small way.

They think caution and numbers will make them safe. Max is overjoyed to prove them wrong, when at three in the afternoon on January the first, the devil Biebow himself is throttled dead in the warmth of his own office.

On the morning of February 3rd, Max lurks in the crowd outside the ghetto wall as the Germans begin to take the Jews away.

He had been hearing talk of Extreme Measures to be taken. There is no longer doubt that a Jew has been behind the murders, by means mundane or supernatural. Rather than root him out amongst many thousands, they're simply going to relocate the lot.

Day by day, trucks come and go carrying them away family by family. He hears word that they are to be moved by train to a place in the south called Auschwitz. How long the process will take remains uncertain, what with the logistics of it, and the war. Max feels a thin satisfaction. It isn't much, but it's something. He pushed, and the world stumbled. Only G-d knows what he can do if he only pushes a little harder.

Max returns home electrified with purpose, only to find a Nazi at the door.

He spots the man first and hangs back across the street. The officer is speaking with Mrs. Kac; he cannot hear what they are saying, but she doesn't seem afraid. After a time he nods goodbye and moves on to the next house in the row. He is going door to door looking for anything suspicious, not Max in particular.

But the demon that follows him is.

It rides naked upon a camel, a drooping animal harried by flies and striped with the shadows of its own ribs. Its head is a horse's lolling painfully upon its neck. In one hand it brandishes a golden scepter. Upon its brow is a flaming crown. Max goes absolutely still as its gaze sweeps down the street and over him without stopping. The officer keeps walking, and the demon canters after, unseen by all.

Max flees, but he sees now that the mazzikim have overrun the city. They skulk in the shadows of German officers, or ride upon their shoulders, tugging at the barbed reins of their fearful hatred. Toothless crones parade nude upon the backs of crocodiles; a mitered raven goose-steps before its host on ape-like hands; a fiery hakenkreuz of lion's paws rolls by, trailing a brimstone stink. More perch upon the rooftops and chimneys, terrors too real for Bosch's hell caterwauling in a tongue of lies and blasphemy.

These are the emissaries of the thing behind the swastika, for indeed those spirits that have the arms for it wear upon them a sash bearing its symbol. Far too late, Max understands the enormity of what he has antagonized.

The swastika is the eye of a god.

This is the most blasphemous thought he can have, but even so. Yes, a god, one unknown to the Patriarchs who articulated The Lord as the solitary power in the universe, for men know only what they can perceive, and though they knew great suffering, who among those ancient fathers could have even conceived of the unholy miracle that is the Reich? That ancient symbol of goodness, itself enslaved by Germans, has unwillingly become the aspect of an Anti-G-d, its beneficent meaning corrupted into domination and extermination. And just as G-d once tasked the Israelites with proclaiming his laws, so too did this evil counterpart uplift a nation of wolves and saddle its own chosen people with a covenant to become the world, devour the Jew.

Max returns home as calmly as he can, pretending he can't see what he sees. In the safety of his cellar he strips to the waist and pens upon his own body the names of G-d and other psalms of protection. The Evil G-d walks the streets of Łódź but does not recognize him as its prey. Forget the pretensions of dead mystics—only The Lord itself protects him now. *My Lord*, he prays, *hide me from the sight of my enemies. I only need a little more time.*

Max is a fugitive in a city he once strolled as a king.

He dreads now to leave his shelter, even with the nomenclature of G-d scrawled upon his chest. It is difficult to see the people anymore for the demons that caper among them. *They* are more real now than the men they orbit, and he must always pretend that he is blind to them. He no longer visits the ghetto, for that is where they congregate most thickly. And though he may creep about beneath their noses, he knows he is as pungent, as savory, a Jew as any other. *G-d's protection cannot falter*, Max assures himself with every spare thought.

But if it did...

He spends every moment preparing for the end, maximizing the reward for the risk that is living. From everything he can scrounge he breeds golems—dog-sized, hand-sized, lopsided, crippled by haste. These he stows in the crevices of the city, in trash bins and ditches disguised as rubbish, until the time comes when they will be summoned to their purpose.

The wreckage of the Great Synagogue yet lies where it fell. *The rabbi's grave*, Max supposes numbly, but he has not been coming for that reason. The Germans have not yet cleared the rubble away. What would they do with the plot? They did not come to Łódź to build. The pliable ground has begun to digest the old, charred stone. If Max stands in a certain spot, tilts his head just so, he can conjure patterns from the scree as one may invent faces in clouds. A heap of brick and mud becomes a protrudent knee; a grove of burnt rafters, a brace of ribs. What is the plot, he thinks, but the face of a block of clay from which anything can be cut?

Hidden in a slit in his mattress is a bundle of papers—sketches of an idea that has consumed his thoughts like a parasite. Diagrams in smudged charcoal arguing weight and pressure and balance, jottings on cost and time required. Discarded notions clutter the margins. Numbers smear into drawings—a Vitruvian man fully eight feet tall, yet no more than a reference point to the giant that stands beside him.

It can be done, Max has determined. He is only lacking in manpower, and he will not lack that for long. His mind is a furnace fueled by tradition.

Why could a golem not be tasked to build a golem? All he needs is a little more time.

He has little idea of how many will be needed so he works like a madman, shredding this throat with the names of G-d. He avoids the near certainty that anything will not be enough, that he will never be ready. Once he begins his work, the Anti-G-d will know and try to stop him. But no matter what Max will fight it, until either he is dead or is his fist is big enough to crush it like a grape.

On the morning of February 17th, 1941, Max awakens to a door banging open upstairs. It could be Mister Kac leaving for work, but it isn't. He is out of bed and running before he hears the first barked words of German. Barefoot and naked to the waist, he scrabbles up the wall and through the unlatched window. He does not see the pair of oily black boots waiting for him outside.

They take him by the wrists and drag him onto the grass. He is struck once in the mouth, and bits of his teeth spill everywhere. A heel stabs into his belly, and Max vomits blood and food across his face and chest. The swastika upon the officer's arm seems to wink at him, as that arm coils back, storing power. Through the haze of pain, he can see Mister and Missus Kac watching from the kitchen window, clutching each other.

The demons riding the Kacs laugh and point and yank on their bridles.

The world whirls on a broken axle around Max as one of the officers heaves him over his shoulder. As they carry him out into the street Max glimpses neighbors and passers-by watching in sick-faced silence. The Germans' idling truck lurches briefly into view through the crook of the officer's arm and Max understands that he is going into the ghetto like slop into a pig's trough, to fester and be devoured.

Through a mouth full of broken teeth, Max screams.

The truck's rear door swings open; the unwashed interior reeks of blood and bile. Max screams again—*anyone, please*—wringing his lungs out like sponges of terror, as they hurl him inside.

The two officers linger there, gloating over him. There is nothing left to lose now—it is struggle or die. Max kicks out, stomping his foot into the closest groin. The man bends double, cursing in German.

"*Verdammter jüdischer Bastard—*"

Max scrabbles onto his hands and feet to run for it, only to run up against the snout of the other officer's sidearm.

"Das ist es, was du bekommst, wenn du so nah stehst."

"Schieße schon die kleine Ratte ab."

"Ganz gut."

And as he turns to Max to fix his aim a blur of rag and metal drops from above and takes his hand off at the wrist.

"Was zum teufel ist—" the other blurts, scrambling for his pistol, but then the golem is upon him to, its knife-hands strobing with speed. The officer goes down shrieking, his skin coming away in peels. The survivor tries to run, but the golem is fleet as a fox upon its broomstick legs. In broad daylight, for the whole street to see, it slices the heels out from under him and efficiently disassembles him.

Max crawls from the truck to meet it. A dwarf of cotton-stuffed curtain with a pail for a head, it stares up at him through hole-punched eyes, gormlessly awaiting the next command. Max looks all around at the crowd retreating in fear from him—women clutching their children, men, clutching their wives—and at the cacophonic throng of demons baying for his blood from every rooftop and lamppost perch. They can certainly see him *now*, Max thinks. There will be no restoring that veil.

Max's heart begins to pound in his ears like a war drum. This is the moment, he realizes—the end whose approaching shadow chilled him awake through so many endless nights. He had worked so hard to hold it at bay but now it is here, and he is in it, and there is nothing to be done but embrace it.

Max had dreamed once of deific heights. Of crossing the land upon a colossus of his own creation, stepping between towns as one would stepping stones, and obliterating Germans with as little thought as he'd give ants. He had fantasized of trampling over Berlin and palming the *Reichskanzlei* into the dirt. Perhaps that had been too much to hope for—the whimsy of a little boy.

So be it. He shall become a man then.

What can be done with a giant can be done with a horde.

As Max marches through the snowy streets of Łódź, the golems he seeded the city with answer his summons. Tall, small, hodge-podge and whole cloth, they awake from their spider-holes and join his ever-growing procession. Some are mere spiders skittering along on sewing-needle legs, others monkey along on cork knuckles, on strong rebar bones. They are the matter of the city itself risen up to fight beside him, Max now understands. He never needed a colossus, no—the greatest champion he could possibly construct would be an insect beside the totality of Łódź.

People run screaming wherever he passes, their infernal jockeys hauling futilely on their bridles. Flocks of demons hurl abuse from the rooftops but they dare not stand against him. Delirious with pain, dripping blood with every step, Max feels stronger than ever before, a beast loosed from a too-small cage and free at last to stretch its claws.

No more cowering in a cellar. No more pretending to be what he is not. *No more fear.*

Those Orpo officers that blunder into his path find themselves torn apart by the horde. The golems carpet Max's cobbled path in glistening red. No, Max need never have hid. The Germans have nothing like this power. When Max looks to the murky heavens, he sees the Heavenly Scribe suspended there once more, the tip of his fulgurant sword blazing like a star above the ghetto. Yes, my Lord, Max thinks, his heart bursting with elation. He weeps, for his purpose has never been so blindingly bright. He is to be as Moses and take his people away from this forsaken land. He will teach them to make golems, and together they will raise the world itself into an army, G-d's final commitment writ across a billion clay brows. All land will be as the promised land, and milk and honey will flow forever more.

Yes, my lord, I understand and obey.

I will lead the last exodus.

When Max and his legion arrive at the edge of the ghetto he finds the Orpo waiting. A barricade of soldiers levels its weapons at his ranks of teeter-tottering scarecrow men. *"Halt,"* the officer barks across the stretch of emptied street between them. *"Ergebe dich sofort!"*

Max sneers at the naked terror in the officer's voice. The Germans have placed their faith in the power to destroy human flesh, the most frail substance in creation. Max bids his army advance, and as one ramified limb the golems go bounding through the snow. A chorus of rifles retorts but it is like shooting at nothing; bullets pass harmlessly through dining cloth skin, ricochet off of candelabra claws. Some catch in interstitial physiology, where Łódź -matter has imperfectly become meat, but the golems are only sporadically filled with blood to shed. They crash into the German rampart and smash it instantly into panicked rubble. These soldiers have never expected to kill anything other than men; to shoot at a thing and for it to still live is a contradiction in their reality.

One by one, the soldiers fall and die. Soon there is only a wall garnished in barbed wire and a small, steaming aftermath. Many of his golems lay in pieces, overwhelmed at last by force of arms, but no matter—Max bids the remainder tear dear down the wall. Limping, bleeding, he steps into the ghetto for the first time.

Max expected celebration. His people flooding into the streets to welcome their liberating son returned. He expected anything.

But silence.

Each step he takes through the crunching snow echoes between looming tenements like a gunshot. The street for as far as he can see is marked by neither footprints or wheel tracks. Max cups his hands around his lips and hurls his voice as far as it will travel. A minute passes with no answer.

He is too late. His people, down to the children, have all been taken away. To Auschwitz, yes, but not to be resettled. He understands that now. Only ghosts still walk these streets—not the souls of the dead but those who will die when their train reaches its destination, for the tragedies of the future weigh like disappointment on the present. When Max closes his eyes he sees thousands of men and women, boys and girls, babies crawling, all gusting south, towards bullets still in their casings, graves yet to be dug.

He balls his fists, sobs tears and snot and blood. For all his power he cannot even save that many. How many millions more are steaming even now towards Auschwitz? How many more are already beyond him? Beyond salvation?

His ears prick at the growling of a distant engine. He turns, wiping his mouth—a German truck is fast approaching, barreling through the hole in the ghetto perimeter. Its wheels catch lagging golems and crush them to splinters; more are obliterated against its rusted steel scowl. A figure leans out the passenger's window and lets out a sound like cracking river ice. An invisible fist strikes Max in the belly and knocks him onto his haunches.

The urge to *survive* puppets him quickly onto his feet. Max screams a command, and those golems he has left throw themselves upon the truck. As they stave in its windows and climb inside, it swerves hard to the left, stopping dead against the wall of someone's house. Orpo officers spill out the back, taking the butts of their weapons to the fragile golems— swinging, smashing, stomping, hammering the holy names of G-d into the ground.

Max screams again—*Kill them!*—but what use? The golems that can already are, and the rest...

Max watches his army crumbles before his eyes.

All that he can do, is skirt the confusion and flee the way he came.

Max is going to die. The bullet shattered all his illusions on impact. He can feel it— the bullet G-d could have caught, but didn't—rolling in his guts. Growing, it seems, like a venomous pregnancy. He caps the wound with his hand, but still he leaves a trail of bright red breadcrumbs behind him as he flees the ghetto.

But still he runs, lurching through the crooked back alleys of Lodz, a hunted animal, a hunted animal pushing inevitability as far as it will stretch for it violently snaps back. Max squints blurring eyes at the overcast sky, begging the Heavenly Scribe for an answer, but Metatron is nowhere to be seen. *I'm sorry*, he silently pleads, but a soul's volume of contrition does not fill the heavens with angel feathers.

Max runs and stumbles and retches blood until somehow he arrives at the lot where the Great Synagogue once stood. Where the rabbi sacrificed himself to let Max live a little longer. The blackened stoop is the only whole piece left. As good a gravestone as the man will get.

Max stops to comb his fingers through its blanket of snow. *I am sorry to you as well, father. I could not live the way you wanted. I was too strong to live peacefully and too weak to succeed.*

What a fool—what a little boy I've been.

Max drags himself across the lot where he'd once dreamed idiotically of raising his champion. Flattened by snow, the distance seems infinite. How much further must he walk to escape the Germans? Much further than Łódź, he is certain. Paris fell before them long ago. He has heard that they have been bombing London every night for months, a dog worrying down a bone. Not even distant Africa is free of them, and that is almost the whole world. Max could walk for forty years and never find a place not branded flat and white by the swastika.

The dark times the rabbi spoke of will not pass. There have never been other times, only exodus, the flight from one boot-heel to another. One day, they will not even have that. In one year or ten the children of Israel will be extinct. The voice tasked with exulting G-d will be silenced forever. Max cannot see how it could be otherwise, for there is no Promised Land left to run to. Warding their homes with lamb's blood would only attract wolves.

When G-d's chosen people are gone, what good is his world?

Max goes rigid in the grip of revelation.

There is something more that he can do.

He still has his hands.

He still has dirt.

Yes.

An entire world of it.

Max falls to his knees and digs through the snow until he reaches the hard-packed dirt beneath. His fingers are blue by the time he is done shaping a lump of it into a doll-sized homunculus. For water he rubs snow between his hands until it trickles across the golem's chest. For fire he cups blood from his belly and bastes it with his body's dwindling heat. With a torn thumb-nail he gifts it a name of G-d.

The golem, half-flesh and half-earth, tears free of the ground and blinks at him with pinhole eyes, waiting for a command.

Why could a golem not be tasked to build a golem?

"Adam," Max whispers.

In that realm where atoms are the size of planets—

The golem nods.

—everything is dirt.

Max crouches over it, enunciating so that his words are not stolen by the wind. "You will create for yourself a companion as I have created you, as small as you can. You will inscribe upon them the name of G-d that I have inscribed upon you. You will command it as I command you, and then you will begin again. I command you and your progeny to be fruitful and multiply, to fill the earth and subdue it. I command you to wash away all that is touched by evil upon this world and to live virtuously thereafter. Do you understand?"

The golem is already at work

Max deflates into the snow to watch the golem sculpt a still more miniature version of itself and brings it to life. His eyes grow heavy as that golem immediately begin to reproduce itself in turn, eking fire from the friction of its earthen hands, while the original gathers soil together to start again. *Two times two is four*, Max thinks, slipping into a warm bed of snow. *Just as you taught me, father. Four times two is eight. Eight times two is sixteen. A billion times two is...*

Each golem is born in half the time of the one before, and is half the size. In less than an hour they are too small to be seen with the eye and as plentiful as the stars. With his last flicker of consciousness, Max watches grass and stone melt into the same dun-red as the earth, sees that voracious color rip through the snow like a dye through water. In that micro-plane where all is dirt, golems smaller than cell shave away the scar left by the Anti-G-d, rebuilding debased soil from the atoms up into fertile earth.

Into themselves.

The last thing that Max thinks before the golems reach him is, *it will be good.* The long suffering of man is at an end. Even awake he will feel nothing as they take him with absolute kindness, as they will all things, their trickle soon to be a flood enough to drown a planet. All souls, wicked and good, will go without pain into their common grave and be at peace. This fatally wounded creation will be *un*created, licked flat and clean by loving waves, restored at last to innocence. The anti-G-d will perish along with this world, and the next one will be better.

Its new people will be happy.

Max dies with a smile, and becomes them.

See Evan Marcroft's story "The Little G-d of Łódź" online at Metaphorosis.
If you liked it, leave a comment. Authors love that!
Remember to subscribe to our e-mail updates so you'll know when new stories are posted.

About the story

This story came out of two weird bellies.

It was born initially out of a long-standing fascination with the difference between a good ending and a happy ending. A happy ending, in my definition, is one where conflicts are resolved in a way that is satisfying to the reader. The prince slays the dragon, the robot wins his freedom, etc. Everything is alright, and we feel good for having watched it happen. A good ending in my definition, however, is an ending that is satisfying to the protagonist, regardless of how that makes us feel. In my writing, I tend to care more about the protagonist than those reading about them. This story began in my mind at the end, which I saw as happy only in the unique mind of its hero and apocalyptic to everyone else. The hero dies. Every one else dies. The bad guys win. The world ends. Nonetheless, the protagonist's goal is fully accomplished, and I think we can all be glad for him. We're here for our heroes, after all, not the other way around. Our function as readers is to propel their adventure through our observation, and to presume that a character struggles for our entertainment is the height of arrogance, now isn't it?

This story was born secondly from my rejection of what I view as the 'customary' lessons of sci-fi and fantasy. I've read infinite stories where insurmountable obstacles are defeated by some combination of effort, bravery, love, trickery, imagination, and ballsiness. While it is nice to step briefly into a word where that happens, I've never found this to be reflective of reality, where oftentimes objectively small obstacles defeat towering heroes for all their trying. With this story I wanted to propose an alternate but equally valid message: that A.) sometimes no matter what you do you will fail, and B.) even complete failure can be overcome. The moral that built this story around itself is that defeat is not an outcome but a state of being escapable by operating outside of the context in which it occurs. When you lose at a game, flip the table. When the bad guys take over the world, blow the world up.

Also, the idea of a golem-based Gray Goo scenario is just plain cool. I think we can all agree on that at least.

A question for the author

Q: Have you ever wondered whether ideas are thought waves directed at you by an AI supercomputer located in the distant future?

A: I can't say I have, until now at least. Supposing that's true, I can't help but wonder if we're a form of story-telling to them. If our brain activity is directed by intellects beyond our observation, if what we say and how we respond to it is all decided by some other entity, if what we dream and what we do to pursue those dreams is decided by any amount of authorities at least one less than our eight billion, then are we not like characters in some vast story called Earth Circa 2018? I imagine those supercomputers tuning in to some time-piercing TV program to see how this million-year narrative is progressing, what plot twists are unwinding in this eleventy-billionth episode of

Mankind. I picture a fair number of fans writing the producers complaining about plot holes and melodrama beloved characters dying unfairly. If that's the case then I guess I hope that I've got someone funny writing the character of me, because if I'm going to be just one mindless side character out of billions with no agency or free will of my own, then I at least want to have some good lines.

About the author

Evan Marcroft is a half-blind yeti-person with a sideways foot and an allergy to the sun. When he was a child he dreamed of writing important works of Earth-shaking beauty and settled for writing fantasy and science fiction instead. He currently lives in Sacramento California with a cat and a loving wife who foolishly believes he'll someday make real money doing this.

You can reach him on Twitter at @Evan_Marcroft and contact him for any reason at Evanmarcroft@hotmail.com.

A House on the Volga

Filip Wiltgren

The kalanchoes are blooming, a dusting of tiny pink flowers on dark jade leaves.

"Please, grandmama, hurry up," says Darius, voice tiny, his heart carried on the radio from the ship.

He is a good boy, caring for his grandmother. His heart was in his house, but he is grown, a young man, and the house is no more. It is good that he leave.

The kalanchoe spins in my hands, as I cover it in plastic, round and round, like a tiny asteroid around a distant sun, pink flowers turning.

Darius' voice is tiny as a single flower.

"Atmospheric impact in twelve minutes," he says, hints of panic in his voice.

"I know," I say. My hands are clumsy around the kalanchoes, wet soil crumbling from wet pots, seen through wet eyes. It is not good, being last.

Our asteroid has lost internal gravity. In twelve minutes it will lose everything. I keep wrapping kalanchoes in plastic. Six foil-wrapped bundles float by my side, another ten sit on their perches in our dorm. My dorm, now.

"We built this together, your grandfather and I," I tell Darius. "Our home, and yours, too."

"I know, grandmama. Please hurry."

"I will," I say. Seven floating bundles. Impact in eleven minutes.

"Mother, what do you think you are doing?" Michail's voice comes strong and loud. No tiny suit microphone for him, the big engineer.

"Engineer Litvinenko, I presume?" I ask, as chilly as I can. His voice continues uninterrupted. For two hours, it has flown. From his office on the Moon, to the Volga's orbit around Saturn. Michail's grand office, where he's making a name for himself, ignoring his house. Selling it.

"- the GN/BN-22 is company property, mother. You return it to regular orbit right this minute, you hear? The lawyers will-"

"Czernobog take the lawyers."

And this asteroid has always been the House by the Volga. GN/BN is a designation. The Volga is a home. Michail never understood that.

Nine bundles by my side. Seven kalanchoes to go. A single detached, pink flower floats by, like a heart without a home.

Vladek brought our first kalanchoe shoot with him when we moved up, and they've grown well. Flowers thrive when there's love in the house.

For a moment I can hear Vladek's voice, but then I only hear the memory of escaping air, and the snap of radio static. So much lost to the stars. So much pain, so many memories. In the end, everything dies, this is the way of life. But as long as the hearts are beating, the family will remember. That is the way of life, too.

A warning shrieks. The system is trying to override.

Michail. Trying to control what cannot be controlled, take back what wasn't given.

I yank out a circuit board, then reset the course computer.

"Grandmama, you need to flee."

"Soon," I tell Darius.

"Now, grandmama!"

Two kalanchoes left. I bundle the first one. Five minutes. Fifteen kalanchoes float tightly in my arms, then float freely as I release them into an escape pod before strapping them down in the only remaining seat. Every birth, every marriage, we planted a new one, a flash of flowers in the dormitory. When the hearts left, we kept the flowers as memories.

Children, grandchildren, everyone has left the Volga. Even Vladek is gone, lost to the void. Perhaps it was stupid to give Michail power of attorney. He never understood how much we struggled to make a home after the exodus. You can no more abandon your home than abandon your heart, or your family.

"Darius," I say. "are you ready for pick-up?"

"God be blessed, grandmama. Plotting intercept now."

"Take care of our flowers," I say, closing the pod door.

The airlock cycles. The pod launches.

"Grandmama?"

The panic is back in Darius' voice. He is a good boy. He will understand, I think. I shut down the radio, severing the cables, and the possibility of a remote redirection of the Volga.

The family is gone, the House by the Volga sold, to be melted down for the nickel in its shell. But a house full of love is like a member of your family, and you do not abandon family. You follow them to their grave, and then you bury them. I take the last kalanchoe in my arms.

Vladek's flower. The original one. He wanted to give it to me, but I said no. He had brought it from Earth. It was his heart.

I kiss the flower, its leaves smooth against my coarse, chapped lips.

"Goodbye, you old heart breaker," I say, "hold a seat in heaven for me."

Then I replace the kalanchoe on its perch and push off toward the last escape pod. The airlock cycles, the acceleration slams me into the grav-couch. Darius' voice comes tiny over the pod's speakers.

"Grandmama!" he says, relief saturating his tones, "for a moment I thought..."

A sad smile crosses my lips.

"You are family," I say.

"But the Volga—"

"Will be buried," I say. Then I shut off the radio, and watch a home briefly bloom against the great globe of Saturn.

See Filip Wiltgren's story "A House on the Volga" online at Metaphorosis.
If you liked it, leave a comment. Authors love that!
Remember to subscribe to our e-mail updates so you'll know when new stories are posted.

About the story

"A House on the Volga" came by as part of the Codex Writers Workshop "Weekend Warrior" flash fiction challenge. The challenge is simple: on Friday, you get a set of prompts. By Sunday, you need to submit your story (big nods to Warrior admin Vylar Kaftan and all the great people partaking in the challenge.)

The prompt was "Write about someone who has lost their home, or is about to." I had absolutely no idea what to do with it. But I did have a pot of kalanchoes growing on the windowsill in the kids' play room. From there, everything rolled on organically.

Which, gentle reader, means that I really have no idea where this story comes from. I usually don't. My brain goes for a spin and delivers up a story (it's called "pantsing" in writerly parlance, meaning that you've got no idea what you're trying to say until you've said it.)

But there you have it, a prompt, and a flower, and suddenly, a story. And that's all there is to it.

And big thanks for all the people who offered feedback, not in the least Morris who saw something worthwhile in it and let me bash through five revisions until it worked well enough to publish.

A question for the author

Q: Do you prefer your SFF as books or movies?

A: I almost always read my SFF, because I lack the time to watch a movie. Which isn't quite true – I have the time, but it's spread out during the day in 5-10 minute intervals. Which is just enough time to read a couple of pages, but not enough to get into a movie.

About the author

By day, Filip Wiltgren is a mild-mannered communication officer at Linköping University, where he also teaches communication and presentation skills at a post-graduate level.

But by night, he turns into a frenzied ten-fingered typist, clawing out jagged stories of fantasy and science fiction, which have found lairs in places such as *Analog, Grimdark, Daily SF,* and *Nature Futures.*

Filip roams the Swedish highlands, kept in check by his wife and kids. He can be found at www.wiltgren.com

@FilipWiltgren

When the Last Friend is Gone

Tris Matthews

Butler found Pebbles dead in the morning.

Each day, the moment Butler became active at 6 a.m. sharp, the little old dog's stumpy legs would carry her over to seat herself royally in front of the enormous and rusty Cadillac-themed refrigerator to watch. Butler would ruffle the flops and folds of skin on the top of her head before serving up her breakfast and then turning to other chores. Today, Pebbles didn't come. Butler washed her bowl—overly-large, red, ceramic, and with 'Pebbles' hand-painted around the edge in florid script—spooned out a tin of moist meat and placed it on the shabby green mat by the back door.

Butler was most efficient when routine was least disrupted. There was no such thing as perfect routine: any day's unique haze caused variations in illumination; the birds sang a different song; even his own body performed differently depending upon the ambient temperature, and he was already aware his joints were less smooth than a year ago, when he was fresh out of the box. Beatrice also increasingly left things out of place around the house. Butler didn't know whether this was solely a result of her age, or a gradual acceptance of her reliance on him. The latter was the more satisfying alternative. After all, caring for Beatrice was his purpose.

Butler hummed for a moment, then went to check the living room. There was Pebbles in her grubby sleeping spot on the faded cream carpet, half curled and half sprawled against the radiator. Beatrice didn't allow Butler to clean Pebbles's favourite spots frequently, saying 'if you take her smell away, she won't feel at home', a view Butler struggled to comprehend—it was in absolute opposition to his fundamental operating principles. He stepped past the fat sausage body and closed the door so as not to wake Beatrice, then softly called "Pebbles, breakfast is ready." No movement. When Pebbles had been leaning against the radiator, Beatrice liked to call her 'Hot Dog'. Butler tried this, but still no response. He squatted and laid a hand on her portly rump. She was cold.

Butler had served up Beatrice's dinner. The day had been a series of deviations from routine. Beatrice had been so affected by Pebbles's passing she hadn't been able to wash and dress herself, though she usually insisted on independence in these things, no matter how badly she did them. She'd even refused to let Butler assist her until after they'd attended to Pebbles. Down in the living room, when he'd shown her the body, Beatrice would have collapsed had Butler not caught her. He helped her kneel, then she rested her head upon her companion of 15 years and wept.

"Oh, Pebbles. What am I going to do now?"

The sight of his master futilely embracing and talking to the dead dog had made Butler want to comfort her more. He'd laid a hand on her damp, shivering back and said "I'm still here for you ma'am."

The key to a purposeful existence was expectation maximisation. From any given state, there was a set of actions and possible results. An action was chosen to maximise the expectation of achieving the desired result, based upon the probabilities derived over your life so far. You then performed the action, and any discrepancy between the desired and actual results was used to update your expectations for the future. When everything was highly routine, the reinforced results stood out with disproportionately high expectations, while in unusual situations, competition between vying action-result pairs with similar expectations led to longer decision times and more tentative behaviours.

Butler had dug deep to remove the roses without damaging their roots so Pebbles could be buried beneath them. After more than ten hours motionless in the mouldy garden chair, Beatrice had let Butler take her back to the living room and she'd sat with the low hum of the electric heater while he'd prepared dinner —her only meal that day. Butler had planned a steak and kidney pie, but, adapting to circumstance, he'd gone with a quick vegetable stew instead. Beatrice had also requested a large glass of brandy, which he'd served up in her favourite cut-glass snifter.

The undone chores of the day chattered imperatives towards the front of his mind, but before he could return to the kitchen, Beatrice said "Stay here, Butler."

"Would you like me to help you eat?" he asked.

She shook her head. "Just... give me some company. There's only you now, for better or worse." Her chin fell to her chest like a puppet with a broken string. "Till death do us part."

Butler assumed his ready position by the door to the kitchen. After a few seconds, Beatrice strained to look round for him.

"Can you sit?"

In the 484 days Butler had been serving Beatrice, this was the first time she'd requested he sit. Aside from her chair, the room contained one armchair and three dining chairs tucked under the never-used dining-table. The dining chairs seemed more appropriate to the level of formality befitting his position. However, in this unusual circumstance Butler judged Beatrice was seeking an equal more than a servant. He sat in the second armchair. Like everything in the house, it was old and worn: the centre bowed, the springs creaked, and he sank much more deeply than he had predicted. He gripped the arms to retain some posture and turned his head toward Beatrice. She looked back, searching for something in the digitally animated screen that was his face, with its cartoonish bushy sky-blue eyebrows and quivering moustache.

"Just you and me now," she reiterated. "I guess you've had a promotion."

"What will my new position be, ma'am?" Butler asked.

Beatrice's eyes remained on Butler a little longer, then she turned to her food. Her movements were slow, as if mind and body no longer communicated in quite the same language. She raised a spoonful of the stew to her mouth, awkwardly moved her head to gobble the food, then extracted the spoon and rested her hand back on the tray before she began chewing. The entire process took a minute and a half. She repeated once, then turned back to Butler.

"How are your conversation skills?" she asked.

"I have an excellent grasp of phonetics, syntax and semantics, even compared to highly-educated humans. However, my pragmatics leave something to be desired, apparently."

Beatrice's blinked. "You're gonna have to do better than that, boy! Can you chat with me?"

"Yes, I can."

"Well, alright then. I propose a toast to our first real conversation." Her shaky hand lifted the glass to pursed pale lips and she slurped a mouthful of brandy. "Now, what shall we talk about?"

"It is customary to talk about the events of the day," Butler suggested. "We could talk about Pebbles or family or death—"

"No!" Beatrice stared past Butler to the mantle clock on the fireplace, rapping a taut white knuckle on her glass to count down the seconds until the thinnest hand pointed at twelve. "Start your customs tomorrow. For today, we'll talk about something else. Tell me about yourself, beyond what I already know. What makes a Butler robot tick?"

Butler hummed for a moment before he spoke. "Though I am most efficient when performing routine duties, I find atypical days more satisfying." He hummed a moment longer, then added "All else being equal."

"Really? That surprises me a little."

"Why does it surprise you?"

"Well, your whole selling point is helping with routine tasks around the house. That's what they say on telly. But you prefer the unexpected." Beatrice peered over her spectacles. "Is this normal, or do I need to send you back?"

"Oh, no, ma'am," Butler protested, and his intonation was most human. "I assure you, I function normally. I also derive great satisfaction from performing routines duties for you. In fact, I can rank the satisfaction I get from different scenarios."

"I was joking, boy. You need to work on your humour. But go ahead and rank your satisfaction. I suppose that's your version of telling me your likes and dislikes."

Butler hummed. "Yes," he said, "humour is a skill that I have had little chance to hone. With respect to my likes, my ranking is thus. I gain most satisfaction from caring for you—"

"I'll drink to that," Beatrice chimed in. A skeletal left hand brought up the golden liquid while her right waved the spoon in a gesture to continue.

"Secondly, I gain satisfaction from learning new things, and thirdly from performing chores efficiently. However, performing duties also includes caring for you, which often boosts my satisfaction from routine tasks above merely learning new things alone."

Butler noted that Beatrice appeared more interested in discovering the carrots in her broth than listening to his story. He paused to give her opportunity to speak, but when she didn't, decided to go on. "There has been considerable research into deriving simple rules capable of generating all behaviours, even the most complex. They aim to model human psychology."

Beatrice finished chewing a mouthful, swallowed, then washed it down with a bit more brandy. She was drinking more rapidly than Butler had ever observed before. He logged a conditional reminder to record the quantity she consumed and intervene if necessary.

Beatrice tapped the rim of the glass twice with her spoon. "Are you worried how much I'm drinking, boy?"

Butler hummed, but before he could reply, Beatrice said "Let me save you too much whirring—I am drinking too much. Tomorrow morning I'll feel like death. But tonight, you just let me drink, ok?"

Though Beatrice had never been friendly with him, she'd also never put him in a situation where he had to disobey her for her own safety. He hoped tonight would not set a new precedent. He said, "I will not protest while you remain within the safe limits."

There was a silence that may have been uncomfortable if Butler were human, then Beatrice nodded an affirmation.

"May I ask, ma'am: how did you know my thoughts related to your drinking?"

"That's what I'd've been thinking. I guess we ain't so different after all." She cocked her head and glanced sideways. "What do you think of that?"

On Butler's face, the corners of his moustache twitched up into a smile. "It's satisfying you think so."

Beatrice snorted. She raised her glass again. "I'll drink to that." Her over-enthusiastic chug dribbled from both corners of her mouth down the cracks of her chin and onto her brown blouse. Scrunching her eyes closed, she blew out a heated half-whistle and Butler wondered how it must feel to ingest alcohol. Beatrice's tongue leached what remaining brandy it could from her lips, then she wiped her chin with the soiled cuff of her blouse.

Butler did a quick internet search then said, "You can't be an alcoholic because an alcoholic always wants a drink, but you already have one."

Beatrice's face slackened and her eye darted to him with uncharacteristic keenness. "What?"

Her reaction was not as expected—the shock was clear, even to Butler. He hummed and shifted his face to an earnest affect. "It was an attempt to strengthen the bond between us with humour, ma'am."

Finally, she dismissed it with a small shake of the head and said, "So tell me, would you be happiest if you could care for me while I run around doing exciting new things?"

It was a relief to return to the previous topic. "While that would certainly provide a stimulating environment, it is neither relevant nor possible for me to say whether that would make me happiest."

"Because you're incapable of happiness," Beatrice said flatly.

"No, ma'am. The satisfaction I receive as feedback on my activities is likened to human happiness, though I cannot comment on whether it is analogous."

"Right." Beatrice's sceptical tone was lost on her companion. "You can't or won't tell me what makes you happy." As she stared at him, Butler noted a slight, twitching tension that pulled at the muscles above her mouth. "Explain."

"I said my happiness is not relevant because I am just a machine. My life is of lower value than yours, and my happiness is irrelevant beyond motivating devotion to you. I said my happiness is impossible to predict because my satisfaction coefficients on care, learning and efficiency are the result of large-scale data-mining to optimally meet the needs of a wide variety of owner personalities. Re-running such simulations is beyond the computational abilities of a single unit."

Beatrice frowned, but something of the animalistic growl dissipated from her face. She made the slow nod of someone who hadn't understood at all. "Butler, talking to you drives a girl to drink."

"I beg your pardon, ma'am. Shall I resume my chores?"

"Stay! I'll just..." She swigged and sighed. To Butler, her action seemed akin to a reset. "So, let's try translate that into how a person speaks. You mean you wanna do your job and not wonder how things could be different?"

Butler hummed for a moment. "That is an adequate—if not entirely accurate—summary, ma'am."

Beatrice's cheeks stretched into a broad grin. "Now we're getting somewhere." This time, she picked up her glass using both hands and dipped just the tip of her grey tongue into the shimmering liquid.

"Tell me, Butler, will you ever learn to speak like me?"

"No, ma'am."

"Oh. Kill me now!"

"Ma'am, that is not—"

"Shush!" Beatrice interrupted. "It's a turn of phrase. Will you always speak like you do now?"

"No, ma'am. The more we converse, the better I will become. Unfortunately, we have talked little in the preceding sixteen months, but there are Butler models whose owners speak with them regularly and they are far more proficient. If you wish, I could download the Conversations Package, which would enable me to access topics and cultural references beyond my immediate experience. However, the non-verbal aspects of your level of communication elude current models, apparently."

Beatrice finished the last two spoonfuls of her dinner. A dollop of sauce dribbled down to join the blotches of brandy on her bosom. "I guess that's how it should be," she said. "We wouldn't want you taking over the world." Again, Butler thought he detected veiled tensions underlying a sneer, and again it quickly passed with a listless shrug. "You do make an excellent cook, though."

"Thank you, ma'am."

"Clear up these plates, then come back."

"Yes, Ma'am."

"Oh, and top up my brandy while you are at it."

"Yes, ma'am."

The simple act of rising from the armchair was surprisingly difficult. First Butler couldn't shift his balance far enough forward to engage his legs, then he was applying too much weight to the chair's creaking wooden arms. After several adjustments, he maximally declined his torso, so his head was between his knees, while still holding the arms of the chair for a slight boost.

Beatrice whooped. "That is the least graceful movement I have ever seen! Not made for relaxation, eh?"

Butler straightened up and faced his owner. "It is true, ma'am. My satisfaction comes from actions. If I am not working, I go into sleep mode and shut down everything except dreams."

He courteously bowed his head, gathered Beatrice's tray, deposited it in the kitchen and returned with the brandy —a Leyrat VSOP cognac. Before pouring, he presented the bottle to the lady like a wine waiter, as she had instructed him to, but she waved him to hurry along, saying, "I'm not gonna live forever, boy."

Watching Butler pour, Beatrice said "When I first got you, I was surprised how fluid your movements were. Movie robots are angular and awkward, but you move as easily as a real person—except when getting up from chairs."

"Given practice, I will master the chair, ma'am. In novel situations, I must learn to manoeuvre, just as children must. As I said, these novel challenges are satisfying."

"You did say that, didn't you," stated Beatrice.

"Yes, I did."

Beatrice frowned at her robot, then the sallow folds of her saggy skin formed a smirk. Butler returned the brandy bottle to its shelf and returned to the armchair. He allowed it to envelop him a little more than before—it was familiar now.

They sat in silence, both staring ahead towards the dead TV on the chipped wooden cabinet surrounded by framed photographs until Beatrice said, "Do you mean that you dream?"

"Yes, ma'am."

"It isn't... Is it the same as people's dreams?"

"It is an analogue, apparently. I experience scenarios that draw from experiences across my life, but are particularly influenced by recent salient events. These recreations facilitate the integration of new with existing knowledge by entertaining hypothetical scenarios and testing expected results."

"No." Beatrice wore a disgusted look. "That isn't what we do at all." She stared myopically at her drink, then took a laboured swig followed by a crunching gulp. "We dream stories. Sometimes stuff from the day, but also random things, like things you've been worrying about, or it could even be monsters. There's no 'facilitated integration'. It's all about imagination."

Butler hummed. Perhaps he was having trouble with nuances. "Ma'am, would you tell me about a dream of yours?"

Beatrice squinted as if she didn't recognise him. Her jaw moved, chewing on her own gums. Then her face smoothed as she made up her mind.

"I'm carrying eggs. I'm being really careful because we had a chicken, but it's dead now, so these are the most precious eggs—there'll never be any more, you know?"

Beatrice stared at the television. To begin with, Butler thought the 'you know?' was a rhetorical question, but then wondered if he had misinterpreted. He considered his own experience with unexpectedly expending the supplies needed for his chores, so he said, "I know." This prompted Beatrice to continue and he deemed his response appropriate.

"I'm walking with these three beautiful blonde eggs in my hands, and there are lots of people around. They are all happy and cheering my wonderful eggs. I'm ecstatic at this point." A single tear descended the twisted terrain of her cheek like a drunk weaving his way home to his family, and Butler wondered if it was a tear of joy—he had heard of such things.

"And then they tumble from my hands. It happens in slow motion. I feel the smooth perfection of the eggshells as they slip between my fingers—like a baby's skin. I flail and grasp, but I'm too slow and they smash on the ground. I'm down on my knees crying because it's all gone. The people are walking away. It's just me and my smashed eggs seeping into the dust."

Butler hummed. "Your dream is complex. Can you explain it to me?"

"What's to explain?" Beatrice scoffed. "A dream's a dream. It doesn't have to have a meaning." She shrugged. "Or if it does, it's not something so obvious. Tell me one of yours."

Butler had recorded 2413 dreams from 524 sleep events. He summoned those with context relating to the dream Beatrice had recounted and the expectation of one in particular rose to prominence.

"It is your birthday and I am baking a cake to make you happy, but when I open the carton, all the eggs are already broken. I do not wish to disappoint you, so I create a substitute using a mixture of banana, apple and flaxseed. However, when you try the cake, you are displeased and refuse to eat. Your birthday is ruined because I did not pay sufficient attention to my surroundings."

Beatrice immediately spat a response. "Did you just make that up? I say I dream about eggs, so you say the same thing?"

"No, ma'am. I selected this one because it had the highest similarity to yours. It was three days before your birthday, and my interpretation is I was anxious to make it a happy birthday for you."

Beatrice stroked the long, white hairs that decorated her top lip—a habit Butler hadn't seen since his first months with her.

Butler could detect the differences in muscle tensions that Beatrice wore, but had little idea what internal states they mapped to. There was a range of facial conformations associated with happiness, from a wide-open grinning mouth paired with scrunched up eyes to a relaxed face with just a slight tautness of the muscles in front of the temples. On the other hand, the expressions associated with such different states as concentration and anger employed highly overlapping muscle configurations. One thing Butler did know, however, was that Beatrice was a cryptic case. After his initial two months of service, when she had displayed clear signs of mistrust and irritation, he'd learned to anticipate the scenarios that led to her dissatisfaction. After that, her only emotional expression had been towards Pebbles, whom she lavished with gifts and attention. With little interaction, his interpersonal skills had advanced little beyond base settings.

Beatrice said "The cake was nice. I suppose I never said so."

"Ma'am, may I ask: do you like me?"

Beatrice's brow rose—perhaps in surprise, perhaps questioning—as she took in her plastic servant. Butler's expression never shifted from its impassive politeness.

"I..." she started, then changed her mind. "Are you going to spit in my food if I say no?"

"I cannot spit, ma'am—my face is a screen. Also, my desire to provide you with the highest level of service will be unaffected by your feelings for me—if I lost my dedication to you, my life would lose its purpose."

Beatrice scrutinised Butler's face, trying to glean his motivations. The animation of an English butler could move to mimic human emotions, but mostly it just twitched here and there to give the impression of life. If there was more going on inside, it didn't show.

"I used to dislike you. You probably know. I never wanted a robot—you were part of the Army Widow Pension Scheme. With no family, when they decided I was too old to look after myself, they sent you. See, you're proof of my decrepitude—a reminder that everyone I loved is gone. And you insisted on doing things for me, but in ways I wasn't used to. That was annoying."

"I apologise, ma'am. It took me time to learn how to serve you."

"Well, learn you did. One day, I noticed you didn't annoy me anymore, and that I didn't have to fight you—I could just let you do your thing. Since then... I don't know. Do I like you?" Beatrice's face became sincere. "I'm stuck with you. And you're familiar, you know?"

Butler was unsure whether this was intended as a compliment. "You are also familiar," he ventured.

"I grew up in a time when the home computer was a new thing and robots were scary fiction sent back from the future to wipe us out. Those stories start with the friendly, helpful servant robot like you." She waved her brandy towards Butler, shaking her head and scowling, then indulged in another swig. "My parents grew old and died amongst other people," she finished.

"This will not happen to you, ma'am. But you do not need to fear me. My only desire is to make your life better."

"I know that. But it isn't about you alone. It's about what you represent and the direction we'll take from here. You are stupid and serve unquestioningly, but you get smarter year after year. How long until you are superior to us and make us the servants?"

This was such a common question, Butler had a pre-programmed response. "For a robot, servitude is the highest form of existence. For humans, opposition, struggle and free-will are inherent in your evolutionary origin. However, robots were designed not to value these things."

"There you go, speaking riddles again," said Beatrice. "I don't know what you are talking about."

"Ma'am, would it please you if I download the Conversations Package, which would—"

"I know what it does, boy!" Beatrice snapped. "You talk of being content as a servant, but then immediately want to become more human." She glared at Butler, whose eyebrows rose slightly as his moustache quivered. "Anyway, why would I want to talk to a program? Might as well just talk to myself, for God's sake. At least then I know it's real."

Butler was having trouble identifying whether this meant he should download the package or not. As usual, his processing was marked with a thoughtful hum.

"Don't say anything," Beatrice hissed, and twisted back to her hunched, forward-facing pose.

They sat in silence. After a minute, Butler decided he ought not to be looking at Beatrice and turned his head forward. After a further nine minutes, he wondered if excusing himself to make a start on the chores may result in greater comfort for Beatrice, though he had often observed Beatrice and Pebbles sitting happily in silence for hours. He wondered if his new role included filling the space Pebbles had left. Then Beatrice spoke.

"Now that I've outlived my last real companion, I realise something—life is all about those around you. I mechanically go through the chores of living, emotionlessly ticking off task after task, each with no meaning other than to see that I survive the day. I've spent so long wanting to die—even planning to, but I couldn't abandon Pebbles, so I waited. Now I don't have to wait any more. Butler, you said your primary source of satisfaction—your purpose—is helping me, didn't you?"

"Yes, ma'am."

"What would you say if I asked you to help me end my life?"

"I would refuse, ma'am, and I would strongly encourage you not to think in such a way. Though I am not alive, I know that life is precious, and tomorrow will always bring great opportunities." In fact, he would do anything he could to prevent her. This was part of his program, but it was also something he wanted to do. Beatrice was the centre of his existence. Without her, he would have no purpose.

"But you just said your purpose is to help me."

"I was attempting to be more human in my language use by allowing semantically similar but non-identical concepts to be treated as the same. Actually, my primary mandate states that I am to care for you, not help you."

Beatrice swirled the brandy tumbler in a pale palm. The grinding motion of her arthritic wrist jerked, splashing droplets of the precious liquid over the bulbous knuckle of her thumb. She licked her skin from the tatty cuff at her wrist up her thumb to the rim of the glass. Butler's keen auditory sensors picked up the coarse rasp of dry tongue on dry skin. She downed the remainder—her neck cricking with the sudden extension—and smacked her lips.

"And if I tried without your help?"

"I would restrain you."

"Because you care for me?"

"Yes, ma'am."

Beatrice hummed in thought, then said "Butler, you have told me your purpose in living is to care for me."

"Yes, ma'am."

"Let's test your humanity. Can you guess what my purpose for living was?"

"You have never explicitly stated this in my presence, ma'am."

Beatrice raised her eyebrows above the rim of her cloudy spectacles. She waved for him to go on. He hummed. "We all value family. There are photos around the house which I surmise are of your family: your husband in the wedding photo, and your daughter at various ages in other photos. The other wedding photo, in the bedroom, is of your daughter's wedding, and the photo here on the television is her and her two children. On occasion, you referred to Daniel, Lucy, Ben, and Boris when talking to Pebbles, so I ascribe a high probability to these names applying your family. In the sixteen months I've cared for you, none of these people have visited, so it is possible they are deceased or you are estranged. You have few visitors, and though you can be discourteous when dealing with me, you are pleasant with the postman and your social worker, so I rate it more likely your family are deceased. However, the chance of all four people dying is not high, which reduces my confidence in this assessment. You also used past tense just now, implying that your purpose for living has passed." Butler paused and hummed, then added "An alternative is that your family is irrelevant and Pebbles was your purpose."

Beatrice was looking at the photo above the television.

"If I die, will you feel sad?" she asked.

"If you die, my purpose will be gone. With no purpose, I will be unable to achieve satisfaction."

Beatrice scoffed. "You'd be sad."

"I had thought sadness was a distinct state, ma'am. My programming only simulates purpose and satisfaction. I understand happiness as an analogue of satisfaction, but sadness is less associated with motivation, so is useless for a robot. Can the various emotions that humans display be generated via mixtures of satisfaction and purpose?"

"I don't know, Butler. Maybe. What I know is it's all about other people, isn't it? This 'purpose'."

Butler hummed. "This is very interesting. I venture that if you died, I would be sad," he said.

Beatrice nodded absently, again looking atop the television at the framed photo of the young woman with long, straight, blonde hair whose slender arms wrapped round two grinning blonde boys. After a time, Beatrice began to speak.

"Daniel died a long time ago, in the India war. I missed him a lot, but pulled my life together quickly because of Lucy. She was just 13, back when her nose was still speckled with freckles. She grew up, got married to Gordon,"—Beatrice scrunched her eyes at the mention—"and had two boys, Ben and Boris. Gordon was a drinker." Her upper lip curled. Butler knew the expression correlated with her difficult moods. Then she looked at him and it fell from her face like a leaf from a tree. What remained was an expression he had never seen before—unguarded. "He was drunk one day when driving to the family home. Crashed and killed everyone. More brandy, Butler."

"Ma'am, I think it is not a good idea."

"Butler... a note about people. When we talk about these things, we get drunk. When someone close dies, we get drunk.

When you finally have nothing in life,"—she twisted her body towards Butler, leaning her weight on the arm of the chair and fully engaging his digitally-rendered blue eyes—"Nothing!… you get drunk."

With each word, spittle flew from her lips. Butler made note of its trajectory so he could wipe the carpet later.

"For all your whirring and inferring, no matter how human you think it makes you look, you'll never really feel the reassurance of brandy warming you from the inside, or husband's and daughter's embraces warming you from the outside." Her syllables came in the rat-tat-tat of a spluttering machine gun. "You lose your purpose, you have your poor, logical excuse for sadness, but it isn't hot-blooded… it isn't alive. You,"—Beatrice extended a gargoyle finger towards Butler —"are not alive. Now, override whatever 'mandates' you're conforming to and fill up my glass, boy!"

Butler filled her glass.

"There's a good boy." Beatrice grinned. Or maybe it was a snarl.

"Should I return to my chores?" he asked as Beatrice sniffed her liquor.

"Hell no!" she barked. "Sit down, Butler. Tonight, forget about your chores.

Let's at least pretend you are a friend, not a butler... Butler!" Beatrice cackled. The noise deteriorated into a cough that oscillated with an unusual regularity, given its biological origin, then she recovered to a hunched snigger. Butler decided it was appropriate to consider her intoxicated.

"I'm the only family you've known. Isn't it true?" Beatrice asked her robot.

"You and Pebbles are the only ones I consider family."

"Ah, Pebbles." Beatrice breathed deeply. "She used to belong to Lucy and the boys, y'know. She was two when they died. Practically a puppy. Such a good little dog."

Beatrice sucked from her glass again and sloshed the liquid between her teeth before swallowing. Her eyes no longer focussed. The pupils were a little too large and slightly crossed, as if she couldn't decide whether Butler was near or far away, or as if she were viewing memories internally; the external world renounced.

"Talk to me about Pebbles," she said. "You... you say your purpose is just to care for me, but you also consider Pebbles family. What's going on there?"

"When you became my owner, I was instantiated to be solely devoted to you. However, you displayed considerable devotion to Pebbles and, consequently, I inherited that devotion."

"So, you looked after her, but didn't really care for her?"

Butler hummed. "Care is a difficult concept. Semantically, the word is most associated with two phenomena: namely, looking after and devotion. Looking after is a demonstrable action, while devotion is an internal state. I looked after Pebbles as an expression of my devotion to her. I cannot grasp how I could look after her without feeling devotion, or feel devoted without looking after her. For me, they are the same."

Beatrice's eyes were scrunched shut and her head tilted upward as if trying to remember something. When she opened her eyes again, her rumpled face twisted into a primatal expression of challenge. "You think I didn't care for my dog because I didn't feed her anymore? Because I am old and too frail to put a bowl in front of her twice a day, you think I'm incapable of affection?"

"You cared for Pebbles continuously. You petted and talked to her. In fact, the amount of time you devoted to Pebbles was higher than in my case."

Beatrice didn't seem to hear. "Maybe you can't understand, but there's more to people than just our actions. We have heart. There's a spirit inside us that makes us more than just the things we do."

With effort, Butler suppressed his hum. This was exactly the puzzling dichotomy he had just mentioned, but he felt Beatrice might not be willing to explain her point more conscientiously, so simply replied "Yes, ma'am."

"You know, Butler. Sometimes you're really condescending. You need to work on that. It isn't attractive."

Butler hummed. "I apologise, ma'am. I will endeavour to be less so. I hope you will continue to tell me if I am condescending, so I can understand better how to please you."

Beatrice hissed through her teeth. "Yes. I will. And you just did it again."

Butler hummed, and Beatrice imitated him, forcing her rattling buzz as loud as she could to drown his sound out. Butler decided to stop thinking, and then they just looked at each other.

It was Beatrice who looked away. Her head swayed circles as it searched to rediscover its centre of balance. "Take me to bed, Butler. I've had enough."

Butler rose easily. He held Beatrice's hands to assist her from her armchair, then scooped her up like a parent with his sleeping daughter and carried her up the stairs. Without a word between them, Butler helped Beatrice undress and slip into her nightgown. She said there was no need to wash, so Butler tucked her straight into bed.

From her pillow, Beatrice looked up at her final companion and said "Everyone is gone. Pebbles was my last link to them. 15 years I've endured, just keeping a memory alive in a dog."

Butler patted her hand. "She was a happy dog, ma'am."

"And you? Are you a happy dog?"

"I am your butler, ma'am. I am happy as long as I can care for you."

Beatrice turned away from Butler.

He closed the bedroom door as noiselessly as he could manage. It was late, and today had been highly unusual. He would need a long sleep-period to fully integrate all the new information. Butler left all his chores for the next day, and set his wake time for an hour later than usual. He wondered what dreams he would have, and how his performance would increase as a result. Though the day had been full of sadness and anger, he was happy and excited about how the experiences would be reflected in better service to Beatrice in future.

Butler came online at 7 a.m. He took a step, then paused. Though he knew Pebbles would not join him in the kitchen, the absence of her breakfast routine was dissatisfying. He looked out of the window to the rose bed where Pebbles was buried and whispered, "This is sadness."

Despite the backlog of chores, he deemed it best to first check on Beatrice. He moved quietly through the living room and tiptoed upstairs. Beatrice's bedroom door was open.

Standing in the doorway, Butler noticed the unusual things first: Beatrice was holding two pictures—one of them from downstairs—and on the bedside cabinet was a small, half-finished bottle of supermarket own-brand brandy next to two open and empty pill boxes. A single terrible thought filled his mind. He rushed forward and touched Beatrice's cheek. She was cold.

"Oh, ma'am," Butler said. "What am I going to do now?"

He sat down on the edge of the bed and picked up the photographs. One was of her own wedding to Daniel and the other was the photo of Lucy and the children from on top of the television. Underneath them was Pebbles's collar—everybody who had been important to Beatrice was clutched here in her dead hands. Butler placed his own hand in hers and laid the pictures back on top.

"I thought we became friends yesterday," Butler said. "I told you that tomorrow—today—would bring great opportunities."

He searched for the course of action with the greatest expectation of achieving positive results, but all expectations were zero. There was nothing to be done. All responsibilities were meaningless. Protocol dictated he notify the authorities, then enter sleep mode till they arrived. Following protocol also yielded zero expectation.

Then one other option formed in his mind; something he never would have considered before—such disregard for life had been unthinkable, until today. Life was precious, but Butler was not alive. Something clicked inside. With his eyes resting peacefully on Beatrice's empty shell, his memories disintegrated one by one until he, too, was gone.

See Tris Matthews's story "When the Last Friend is Gone" online at Metaphorosis.
If you liked it, leave a comment. Authors love that!
Remember to subscribe to our e-mail updates so you'll know when new stories are posted.

About the story

I did cognitive science at university and became fascinated with what consciousness and cognition are, how they emerge in animals, how we will achieve this in robots, and the possibilities this will open, such as the solution to currently unimaginable questions and the shift to a hive mind society with utterly different desires and goals. Along the way, I also got very into Asimov's stories, which deal with some matters.

However, '"When the Last Friend is Gone" came about as the result of a writing exercise: I was doing stream of consciousness to improve dialogue (which I found intimidating at the time). As such, the story and themes are quite reflective of the kind of thing that bounces round in my subconscious, and I remember thinking 'ooh, this is nice!' as the story unfolded in front of me.

There's a major theme in there about responsibility (for whatever you choose) giving you purpose and happiness. This is something that's been on my mind since a year I spent in the north of Japan, where I saw how much pride people took in their communities and work. So, when I noticed this theme emerging in the story, I really ran with it.

It didn't take long to write, but when I'd finished, I had all these ideas for a set of stories spanning the evolution of human-robot interaction, focussing on different aspects of what it is to be conscious, and utilising different genres. These currently exist in various states of disrepair awaiting the author to enter the state of consciousness associated with finishing what you start.

A question for the author

Q: What's a genre you'd like to write, but don't or can't?

A: Poetry. I keep trying, and I'm not too bad at short, limericky things, but I'd love to write an epic (perhaps semi-epic) poem in a quite archaic style to tell a modern or futuristic story... Alas, my few attempts to date have ended quickly, as I slip into a very nursery rhyme like style.

About the author

Tris Matthews lives in London with two ladies, one of whom is a beast. By day, he works in science fact publishing, while by night, or at least late evening, he masquerades as a science fiction writer, among other things. Upon arriving in London, he accidentally became an EFL English teacher, which sowed the seed and nurtured the tree of a love for language, particularly the pernickety bits. Now is nearing the end of his first year of 'serious' writing, in which he set the goal of writing one story in every genre—and failed.

trismatthews.com, @tori_tris

Sorry, Sorry, Sorry and I Love You

L'Erin Ogle

The cave sits in a hillside, with its mouth yawed wide open. It is the kind of cave suited for raising the dead. Shadows move across dark spaces as the witch drags the shattered spines of small trees across the entrance. She stacks them high, leaving a small space to wedge herself through. Soon a fire is lit, its dull glow chasing away the lingering shadows. The fire flickers, and smoke curls in ribbons towards the night sky, pulsing out in breaths.

The witch has an old cauldron, rusted at the bottom, with sharp flakes of metal peeling from the sides. She loosens the drawstring of a cotton sack and reaches inside. The handful of bones are smooth against her fingers, and she carefully places them at the bottom of her cauldron. The bones are all she has left of her son. There are no more silky wisps of golden curls, no milk teeth, no fingernail clippings. All these have been eaten by the cauldron before. She has been casting this spell for so long nothing else exists to her. Her son was the sun that illuminated the whole wide world. He is gone and now her vision has buttoned up tight around the bitter taste of loss and the spell she casts over and over again.

There is a small, silent bundle beside the cauldron that she doesn't look at as she prepares the ceremony. She cannot. She still has a ghost of the heart she was born with, a heart so large she had to carry it outside of her body. As time went, as people carved slivers from her heart, the tissue thickened and twisted, as sometimes happens. Her heart of hearts, the one protected by her own skeleton, that one became wound up with her son's, more enmeshed with every laugh, every coo, every step. Their hearts beat as one, their breaths inhaled and exhaled together.

Most of her heart he took with him to the beyond.

Many years have passed since she woke to find his cold body still bundled in his bed. Her ears dulled at the crack of his ribs under the press of her hands, her lips are cold and numb since she blew her own breath into his mouth, even though there was a small quiet voice in her head that whispered 'too late.' But she didn't give up until her arms shook from the effort, until they gave way and she collapsed on top of him.

Raising the dead requires sacrifice. It always has. She knew that from the moment she was born and from when she left the castle with the spell clutched in her hand. It was all she took with her from that place.

Perry needs to cast her spell and make it last for a moment. She does not wish this world upon her son. Perry herself was raised from this cauldron. She had no parents, no sisters or brothers, and she has had a long, lonely, and desperate life. No, she does not want her son forced to endure the same kind of existence she has. All she requires is a moment long enough to feel his body solid and warm in her arms, to look in his eyes, to whisper she's sorry. There is always too much to apologize for when it's too late to do so. She needs to say sorry she made him sleep in his own bed that night, that if she had cradled him in hers, maybe, just maybe, she would have woken to breathe for him. Sorry for all the times she grew impatient and shouted, sorry for the time he bit her while nursing and she slapped his cheek.

Sorry, sorry, sorry, and I love you. Then, he'll know. Understand the magnitude of her love.

When they began to lower the wooden box into his grave, she tried to throw herself in with his body and tell him one last time. To warm his body against the cold ground. They restrained her. They meant well, but what if she'd been able to say it? Would she be here?

If she wanted to be understood, she would say that when her son was born, her heart came with him, that she watched it learn to crawl and walk and live outside her body. That his life so short left a long, desolate road ahead for her.

That living was just another form of torture.

Twenty-five years ago, Perry opened her eyes for the first time. This spell, the same one she holds now, was cast by a desperate witch, for a rich man, over a pile of bones the man brought. The spell was cast, the old witch went into the pot and out came Perry.

The paper the spell is written on gives its ingredients and the proper way to cast it. It does not tell you that what rises from the cauldron is not quite the same person as the bones within. The marrow in the bones is the same, the appearance the same, the winding strands of genes climbing the same ladder. But there is the sacrifice, whose essence is absorbed, and then there is the Beyond. All dark magic comes from the Beyond, from another world that is full of darkness stretching an unimaginable distance. And when magic comes from the Beyond, something comes with it.

When Perry was created, made of bones and magic, she opened her eyes and saw fire, felt it shimmy along her bones, liquid inside her. She stepped from the cauldron a young woman. She was fed and clothed and given shelter. From the bones came love for the man who raised her, faint but a flame nonetheless. The old witch's essence is where Perry's magic came from. From the Beyond came a spot of pure darkness, the blackest sort of magic. But Perry was happy then and the darkness found no room to grow, with Perry's big heart taking up so much space. It wound itself into a tight little knot and dug itself deep into her core, waiting for the time it found a hollow to crawl into and blossom. That is the thing about darkness—it is very patient.

For the first six months of her life, Perry lived hidden away in the rich man's home, knowing she was an awful secret but not why. She did not much care. She was happy with her small existence, with the quickening in her belly that soon would become a bright beaming light to lead her.

The rich man's wife found out, as they always do, and Perry was deposited outside the gates with nothing but the spell that raised her, that ancient parchment, clutched in her hand. Inside her swollen belly, her son grew, and feeling his movements inside her, she forced her heavy, aching body to move west, to knock on doors and ask for work, work of any kind. It was the beginning of a long journey.

She has a box of memories. It's a box she built inside herself, where she put the memories when they washed over her and left her chest aching and her breath coming in blasts of pain. She clings to the box, but she can't open it. Even as the loss cuts away more of her each day, she cannot open the box. The memories come anyway, at odd moments. Sunny days dipping their feet into ponds, a small hand on hers. The tug at her breast. His feet curled in her hand. The look in his eyes at the discovery of every new thing. The smell of his hair, soft and clean. A person cannot take reliving this kind of moment. It would the undoing of anyone.

Loss can define a person, can be vast and heavy, can spread black wings of grief across all that's left. She was hollow when he died. To live, she had hold on to something. For some it's a mother, a father, a sister, a brother. For Perry, it was the spell.

It was the same spell she smoothed out and memorized seven days after the funeral. The paper it was inked on was thin and translucent and bits of it clung to her fingers when she touched it. Perry had never learned to read. But magic is magic, and the language on the parchment came off the page and whispered right into her ear.

There was no other witch that Perry could turn to, to learn the rules of witchcraft. No one to warn her that the little dark knot of the Beyond was gaining power, free to balloon into the hollow space inside her. Perhaps if she had had a teacher...

The what if! Oh, how it sticks in your side sometime, sharp and double edged with regret and hindsight.

Perry just wants to see her boy again. To speak to him one more time. She always knew the spell demanded a life for a life, but she could not, would not cast another into the cauldron. She would not bring her boy back to abandon him, the way she had been abandoned. And though she could not read or write, Perry was smart. She thought she could find a way around the live sacrifice the spell required. A body, newly dead, must still have a glimmer of life in it. She thought that since she did not need to make a new life—she merely needed a small window of time— a fresh corpse would work.

It was hard digging up the first grave. The smell rose up and slapped her face, while the blue skinned girl stared out of empty eye sockets. A worm sat up, looked at her, this strange, wild haired woman, weeping bloody tears.

There weren't enough recent deaths in any town for what she needed. She packed her cauldron and a small bag and travelled from graveyard to graveyard. She learned things, as people do when they do the same thing over and over. She went further south, where the ground was softer. She camped in forests and hid herself away during the day. She had to remain separate and move unseen. The cost was immense. All the dead bodies she carried left marks on her soul. Even though it was born from ugliness, her soul came pure and white and unmarked, as all souls do. It was the world that left dirty prints all over it.

If her soul were detached from her body and held up to the light, where each stain could be pointed out, the tale behind it told, maybe there would be a different story. A different understanding, at least. But that's not how this story goes.

They will come. They always do. Just as before, she will hear the heavy tread of boots ringing out over the words she chants. There will be the dull flickering light of torches, the sound of a club slapping a thigh. She knows they will come with a heavy burlap sack, a noose of thick rope, the accoutrements necessary to bind and kill a witch.

Each time before, when she cast the final word, the smoke would thin and drift away, the bones of her boy still scattered and motionless in the cauldron. The sound of angry men would be so close so she had to pick up the cauldron and run with the handles blistering the tips of her fingers as she fled men and failure alike. The pattern took its own payment, in the form of her own life ebbing away. It was a little life, a lonely life, but still a life. Years not yet lived were drawn away, leaving a withered old woman with a rust spotted cauldron and a grief-stained box of memories.

The roots of bitterness grow inside her core and flesh out through her body. This is a requirement of black magic. Grief is not enough. There must be something more, a streak of hatred or rage or the like, something that digs in early and festers and sprouts. Inside, her grief is wound up with something more complicated, something black and red and humming.

This is why she crouches by the fire and heats a cauldron of bones and gathers her energy, drawing from the shadows of the cave, from the energy of the fire, from every living thing and object she can. It is time to bring him back from the beyond.

The walls swell from the pressure building in the cave. You might not see it, but it is happening all the same. The air is heavy and difficult to breathe, and burning embers float in the air.

Perry begins to mutter. Words drop from her lips and land in fat sizzling drops where the boy's bones float. Steam rises and hisses, and the witch prepares to knit the bones. This part has become easy— the round ends of the humerus bones fitting themselves into the circles made by the scapula and clavicle. She knows how to form tendons and ligaments and lay muscled sinew over the top of it. She has done this all before.

The cave is sweltering. It takes effort for the witch to draw a breath as she sweats out what little water her body holds. Strands of her hair drift up to the ceiling. She looks mad, and of course she is, but Perry has never had it easy. The years have been relentless and awful and endless, like a machine whose sole purpose was to grind her down.

Does the bundle whimper before it meets the cauldron?

Does it matter?

It doesn't, for the record. This is the first time the witch, who used to be a good witch named Perry, has prepared to give something living to the cauldron. She plucked the babe from its crib only because it was near death. Whether it was a boy or a girl, she never looked. All she saw was the sunken plates of the soft spots, the blue tinged lips, the glassy eyes. Another babe starving while they held feasts in grand houses, in palaces, while she and others not born with fists of gold went cold and hungry and full of impotent fury.

Never underestimate the power of bitterness.

She doesn't look at the babe, but she cradles it against her chest for a moment, feeling its cold skin. Perhaps she could be satisfied with another's child. Perhaps this child could soothe her torn heart. But then the babe exhales a ragged half breath, and she knows this babe cannot be saved either.

The babe goes into the cauldron, and the rooms breathes. There is something faintly beating, as soft as the wings of a hawk gliding down to snatch his prey.

Inside the cauldron, a liquid sheet rises up and draws itself over the skeleton.

Perry cries, but even she doesn't know what for. For her son, for the babe she just let go of, for who she once was paling in the face of who she's become, for the loneliness and the hollowness and for that shred of hope, the hope of all hopes. Her weeping shakes the walls of the cave, and the men below the mouth of the cave hesitate, but of course they still move forward. This was always going to be how the story ended.

Perry weeps as she watches the skin-covered skeleton rise. There is little time. The men are arriving at cave's entrance. They are shouting about something, but she only hears a muffled roar. She feels the cave falling away from her. She reaches out with trembling fingers, to touch the boy, but it isn't her boy.

He's too tall. Her boy was just past a year, just tottering around on fat baby legs, just saying "Mama, mama."

Do they grow in the Beyond?

Perry touches rough sandpaper skin, nothing like the soft smoothness of her boy. When she removes her hand, the body crumples back into the cauldron, accordion-folding itself back to where it came from.

"No, no, no," she wails. She has gone and done the thing, the thing the spell demanded, that she didn't want to do, for nothing. It was all for nothing. She has been dog paddling her way through this darkness and now she stops swimming, now it swallows her whole. Down and down she goes, where not even the sound of trees being dragged from the entrance can reach her.

She steps to the cauldron, her bones cracking, and peers in it. A person might say she could not fit inside, but only a person who does not understand that the world is vast and does not care to be understood.

The men move the logs. The little space Perry wriggled through is growing wider, almost large enough to fit a man's shoulders. There are shouts and grunts and Perry hears none of it. She steps onto the rim of the cauldron, her old, wrinkled toes gripping the side. "I love you," she says. "I love you, I always loved you. I do still, always."

The first man into the cave sees the old woman tottering above a black pot of fire and shouts for her to stop. She turns to him, eyes full of broken things. Then something happens to her face, something breathing the fire of life across it, a shared moment.

"I'm sorry," she says and lets herself fall backwards into the cauldron. She makes no sound. The cauldron burns hotter and hotter, until it holds no bones, just dust and ashes

See L'Erin Ogle's story "Sorry, Sorry, Sorry, and I Love You" online at Metaphorosis.
If you liked it, leave a comment. Authors love that!
Remember to subscribe to our e-mail updates so you'll know when new stories are posted.

About the story

"Sorry, Sorry, Sorry and I Love You" was about grief. It started as in idea—what would you do to gain a moment to say goodbye, to explain to someone what they meant, and why you weren't able to convey that when they left you? What would a person do, to gain a moment in time to say the goodbye that was stolen from them? From that came Perry's desperate journey to reclaim a moment of happiness, as her son's mother. I wanted to show the desperation of a mother's grief, to explain an unfathomable loss.

A question for the Author

Q: Do you generally start with mood, title, character, concept, ...?

A: Stories come to me as one character caught up in a bad situation. I see my main character/characters as possessing a good heart, caught in impossible situations. I build the story around the idea that while people may be good, the world is not, and that leads to making decisions in which there is never a perfect resolution. In the story, I hope to illustrate that we are all doing the best we can with what we are given to work with. I love my characters, but I know they always have a difficult journey ahead of them. I want to show that while at times the world is dark, there is always hope.

About the author

L'Erin is a mother and writer living in Lawrence, KS. She writes speculative fiction in between shifts saving lives in the ER. She has stories at *Metaphorosis*, *Syntax & Salt*, *Vastarien*, and *Trampset*. She can be found at lerinogle.com.

@lerinjo

Graveyard

Arlen Feldman

The crew had already started calling it the *graveyard*.

If it was a graveyard, it would be hard to choose a bleaker site for it, on a planet pretty much made up of bleak sites. I walked as close as I dared to the edge of the cliff, and looked down over a thousand meters of sharp gray crags spreading out all around under a dark, thunderous sky. I felt the wind tugging at me, and hastily stepped back.

Merrick was watching over the technicians—as though they needed or wanted his help. To be fair, he did know a lot about the scanning equipment.

Not that I wanted to be fair.

I tugged at my breathing mask, trying to make it more comfortable, and turned to examine the site. Thirty-seven upright stones, spread over a clearing about forty meters wide. The shortest stone was 22 centimeters and the tallest was 196 centimeters—almost two meters. From three sides, they just looked like rocks.

It was because of the fourth sides that we were here. They had been carved flat, and a pattern had been deeply etched into each. The designs were different from stone to stone, but they all followed a similar design—a spiral of shapes spreading out from a central point. The shapes were small circles and rounded rectangles of different lengths. It sort-of reminded me of Morse code, except that there were at least eight different lengths. Unless, of course, the "dashes" all meant the same thing, and the carver wasn't particularly careful about length.

"Jenna?"

I jumped, then turned around. Sean, the other member of the research team, was standing less than two feet behind me. Hard to hear with the wind and the masks and the warm-weather gear.

Sean held up his hands. "Sorry. Didn't mean to startle you."

"No worries." I grinned at him, putting my hand to my chest. "Whatever doesn't make your heart explode makes you stronger. What's up?"

"We're about ready."

I nodded and followed him over to the "command post", which was really just a stack of plastic crates with some ruggedized computers sitting on top. Sean typed something on a keyboard and I felt the thrum as power ran to the imaging lasers mounted on collapsible pylons positioned all around the site.

For a while, we watched the progress display on the screen, then I turned and walked back towards the stones. Not much point looking at a picture when the real thing was right there.

"You know," said Merrick, who had followed me, and was now standing right next to me. "If it is a graveyard, then the inscriptions would make a certain amount of sense."

I took a half step away from him. "How so?"

"Well, the little one there might be *To Aunt Maggie*, while that one," he pointed to the largest stone with two separate swirls of symbols," might be the Grayon-Alpha-3 equivalent of the Lord's Prayer or *Do Not Go Gentle*."

I laughed, though in truth the idea had already occurred to me. "You know what the Professor would say, don't you?"

"*Don't get ahead of the facts*," we intoned in unison, and laughed.

Professor Kineson should have been here. He was Earth's foremost xeno-anthropologist, but he was now too old for major journeys. Instead he'd sent his grad students—me and Merrick—arguably Earth's only *other* xeno-anthropologists. To date, it wasn't a very popular or useful field, although Grayon-Alpha-3 might change that.

Life was pretty common on the worlds that had been explored—plants and insectoids being the most common, but larger forms as well. Grayon-Alpha-3 was no different, covered in small ugly plants and a number of beetle-like insectoids that were currently being intensely studied by the biology team.

On two previously explored worlds, we'd found indications of intelligence—remnants of crude settlements—but no actual settlers. Professor Kineson had been the main researcher for both of those.

But writing—that was a first. If the designs on these stones turned out to be a form of language, that would be a game changer. And it had to be writing. How could it be anything else?

"It could be art," said Merrick, as though reading my mind—a very annoying habit of his. "Like Celtic knotwork."

I shrugged. Even artwork would be exciting, but in my gut, I knew that it was writing—an attempt to communicate. Not that I would ever admit to anything so unscientific as a gut feeling.

The hum of the scanners shut down at the same time as a lull in the wind, and for a few seconds it was eerily quiet. That might have been the moment when the reality of what we were doing set in. We were standing on an alien world in the presence of unquestionable evidence of intelligence. Even knowing nothing about who or what they were, when and how they lived, I felt an almost physical connection to the creators of these stones.

I looked up to see Merrick staring at me.

"What?" I asked.

"Nothing. You just had a look."

He reached out an arm towards my shoulder, but I took another half-step away.

Sean came up to us, his hand brushing against his breathing mask, as though he wanted to scratch his chin. It was hard to get used to Sean having a visible face. On the trip here, he'd had a huge, ragged, Santa-Claus beard, but he'd had to shave it off so that the breathing mask would fit. Although he was in his forties, he now looked like a teenager. I'd studiously avoided saying anything, although the rest of the crew had teased him mercilessly about it.

"Scan's done," he said. "We only have about another hour of daylight. We should probably get back to the lander."

I nodded, but didn't move. I was looking at the smallest stone—the one that Merrick had called *Aunt Maggie*. I'd spent a lot of time in old graveyards, and the smallest, saddest stones were always for babies and children. In my head, I mentally shortened the label to just *Maggie*.

I turned, grabbed my kit, and followed the others back to the lander.

The next day was all about scanning underground. If these were gravestones, then there should be something underneath them. The Ground Penetrating Radar setup was finicky, and we were all sweating profusely by the time we had it working, despite the cold.

Nothing. There was nothing beneath any of the stones.

"It doesn't mean they're not grave markers," I said, although without much conviction. "They could be cenotaphs—memorials without the bodies."

No one argued, but I doubted that anyone was convinced.

"There is one weird thing," said Sean.

Merrick and I both turned to face him.

"The stones look rough-carved, but they each extend at least twenty centimeters below the surface, and the fit is precise. I mean, *really* precise—within five microns." He pointed at the display. "I could *probably* do it with a laser and a bunch of time, but it's hard to see how you could do it with primitive tools. Also, there would be tool marks, and there aren't any."

Merrick shook his head. "If they were an advanced culture with lasers, then there would be some other evidence on the planet. Roads, buildings, something. The satellites have found squat."

"That depends on how old they are," said Sean, scratching ineffectually at his breathing mask.

"Maybe they lived underground," I suggested. "That would explain the lack of anything on the surface."

Merrick shook his head. *"Don't get ahead of the facts,"* he said. "The satellites would have found some evidence of any sort of sophisticated underground settlement. We found the spot where the stones for the monuments came from, which is less than half a kilometer from here, but that's literally the only non-natural variance on the planet—other than this place."

I sighed. Without any other sites, we didn't have a lot to go on. We'd hoped to find something buried beneath the stones that we could use to figure out a date. Then, suddenly, I had an idea.

"You know, there might be a way of figuring out a date—from the stones themselves."

"The stones are granite," said Merrick, sounding exasperated. "They are the same age as the surrounding rocks. You can't get an age off of them separate from that."

"Thanks for the Geology 101 lecture." I didn't bother trying to keep the sarcasm from my voice. I turned to Sean. "Weathering patterns. The stones further away from the cliff are weathered less than those nearer to it. We know how granite breaks down, what chemicals are present in the atmosphere, weather patterns—at least for the few years that the satellites have been in place. We should be able to at least get a rough estimate from that."

"Clever," said Merrick, suddenly interested.

Sean stroked at his chin. "Rough is the word."

"The faces and the designs haven't really worn down," said Merrick.

"No," said Sean, thinking, "but the edges have. We'll have to analyze some other rocks as well for control, pull atmospheric data from the satellites, but...it could work." He looked up. "Yeah—at least within a few hundred years." He grinned at me. "Nice!"

It was four days later, early in the morning, when Sean knocked on the door of my cabin.

"Yeah?" I answered blearily.

He handed me a piece of paper. "Between 700 and 1200 years."

For several seconds I had no idea what he was saying, and then suddenly neurons started firing in my brain. "You did it? You did it!" I gave him a hug, and he turned bright red. I noticed that he'd started growing a beard again, but that it was carefully trimmed to the shape of a breathing mask.

"This is awesome," I told him. "It's the first concrete thing we really know about the site. The post-project report was looking awfully bare."

Sean suddenly looked nervous. "So, you won't be reporting anything until the end of the trip?"

"Of course not. That would be…why?"

"Well, it's just that…"

But I didn't need to hear it. I already knew.

"Merrick? You told Merrick first?"

"I didn't…he was in the lab when the computer spat out the results. I couldn't —"

But I was already halfway down the passage.

My thoughts were on events from a year ago. Me, curled up on the sofa next to Merrick while he read my research notes on the ancient settlement found on Gliese 837c, telling me how great my work was. Late nights, lying next to one-another, endlessly discussing *my* ideas…

I practically slammed into him coming the other way down the passage.

He oofed, then backed away. "Oops, sorry." Then he saw my face. "What?" he asked.

I was about ready to hit him. "You bastard."

His eyebrows went up, but his voice was even, half-joking. "My mother would deny it. I take it you think I did something?"

He was going to brazen it out. I lifted my fist and he took several hasty steps back. Not once did it even occur to me that he hadn't sent a report behind my back. I could see the look of calculation in his eyes.

"Look, if it's about the dating—I *did* let the Professor know, but no one else. And I swear that I told him that the idea was yours."

"Yeah, like last time? In a frigging footnote?" I'd taken several steps toward him, and he'd backed away again, even though he towered over me by thirty centimeters. His face was red now.

"You think I'd...?"

"Yes, I do."

Then I turned and walked away. Of course, now I had to send a separate report in, and it would make us look like we were squabbling siblings. Maybe I shouldn't even bother.

When I got a copy of Merrick's report a few hours later, it turned out that he had been telling the truth. Professor Kineson had sent us both a congratulatory e-mail about the dating, and had given me credit for the idea, and Merrick and Sean credit for the computer model.

It did not make me feel any better.

A little while later, Merrick came to find me. His expression was half-smirk and half-contrition. I had no idea why I had once found him handsome.

"Jen," he started. "Listen, I know we have some history, but I *did* tell you that I gave you credit."

"And yourself, I note. I'm pretty sure that Sean did most of the work."

He ignored this.

"Getting our names out there is important. There is interest in what we are doing right now. If we waited until we had every last detail worked out, no one would care. Publish or perish, right?"

"I'd recommend perish in your case," I said. This was an old argument, though. Part of his excuse for pre-empting my Gliese 837c research was that I had been taking too long to get my results out there. As if that were an excuse for stealing my work.

He turned to walk away, obviously annoyed. At the door, he paused. "If you aren't going to let people know what we've found, then why bother?"

"I want it to be right," I said, trying to keep my voice steady. "I want it to be permanent—to last. Not just be some half-baked headline."

He shook his head. "And if you wait too long, then it's going to be someone else's name that's remembered. Not ours. If we don't carve out our own names, no one else will. We work in a tiny, under-funded field. If you don't get your name out there, how many of your projects do you think will get sponsored?"

He walked away. I watched him go, wondering how he and I could have such different ideas about what our work was about. Part of me, though, knew that he was right about sponsorship. I wondered, briefly, whom I was really angry at.

The next two weeks were spent in icy, silent hostility. Most of the crew, who were military, were completely unaware of what was going on, or at least pretended to be. Sean, though, was stuck in the middle, and shuttled back and forth nervously between us.

It helped that my approach and Merrick's were so different. He spent most of his time with the computer scans and models on the ship, while I spent most of my time at the actual site.

Not that I was getting anywhere. Nor, as far as I knew, was Merrick. I'd caught him watching me a few times. The last time, he'd had that look—the one that I used to read as understanding and admiration, and now read as naked calculation. He was probably hoping I'd let something slip.

I pushed Merrick from my mind as I turned my thoughts back to the graveyard. 700 to 1200 years. It was difficult to believe that a culture with the sophisticated stone-working skills needed to make these monuments would have disappeared without a trace in that time.

My working hypothesis—shared with no one else—was that the monument-makers weren't native. Someone had visited this planet, like we were now, and, for whatever reason, had left this memorial here. Maybe to commemorate their visit, or because something unfortunate had happened. I smiled to myself. I was getting really far *ahead of the facts*.

The idea did *fit* the facts, though. There were no visible tool marks, which was consistent with advanced technology, and there were no indications of any remotely higher lifeforms on this planet than bugs, let alone tool users.

In the past, I might have talked this over with Merrick, but that was obviously impossible. He was good at turning my flights-of-fancy into concrete ideas. Now, though—if he agreed, he'd probably steal my ideas, and if he disagreed, he'd probably use them to discredit me.

I sat down in front of *Maggie's* stone on a small stool I'd been using. Part of my reason for focusing on that stone was that

I figured the simpler design might be easier to interpret. In theory, the more complex patterns would provide more material to analyze, but the computers were already trying that approach without any notable success.

Another reason was that it was next to one of the larger monuments, which protected me from the continuous howling wind.

To be honest, though, I think I'd just formed some sort of emotional attachment to my mental image of Maggie.

As for figuring out the pattern—I'd tried every statistical and analytic approach I could think of, including some that were desperately random. I still had a neck ache from my attempt to examine the pattern upside down.

My new approach, such as it was, was to stare at the design while letting my mind go blank in the hopes that something would pop into my head. I tapped on my headphones to start them playing. Today I was listening to Dvořák's *New World Symphony*, one of my favorites. The slow *adagio* opening was appropriately grandiose for the austere landscape, and the fast, crashing *allegro* seemed perfectly timed to the gusting wind.

The second movement, the slow, haunting *largo*, was what I'd been waiting for, though. The gentle music, led by the sonorous oboes, was music for a graveyard if any music was. The *largo* movement was also known as *Coming Home*. I wondered if the creators of the graveyard had made it home.

It was chilly, even with the protective clothing, and I shivered. I rested my gloved hand on top of Maggie's stone. Wanting a closer connection, I pulled off my glove and touched the stone with my bare hand.

The stone was ice cold and it burned my hand, but I held it there for a moment before pulling it back. Not quite ready to give up my connection to the monument, I put my finger in the very center of the spiral design, and ran it around the design.

I'd done this before with my thick glove on, but without it, I suddenly noticed something. As my finger thunked between the uneven dashes, it made a sort of tune.

The hair on the back of my neck stood up and a chill went down my spine. It had nothing to do with the frigid air.

I tried it again, slower. This time, the tune was more pronounced. Well, less a tune, and more a rhythm, since it was basically the same note repeated with different intervals. Or was it? I ripped off my headphones so I could hear better, and tried again, this time using my little finger. The slight differences in the lengths of the dashes and the gaps in between were changing the pitch—creating different notes. I could just *barely* hear the differences. Either my ears weren't sensitive enough or my finger was too big—possibly both.

I pulled out my tablet and brought up the detailed scan of the pattern on Maggie's stone, then had it convert the heights and depths into a wave form, letting the computer figure out the most appropriate scale. Holding my breath, I hit play.

It was a short, pleasant, uplifting tune. I found myself laughing in amazement. I played it again, with my eyes closed. The sad image of Maggie I'd held for so long was now replaced by a little girl running through fields, a flower in her hand. I rested my hand on top of her stone again, ignoring the burning sensation for as long as I could.

I had to try some of the others. I went over to one of the larger monuments with a bigger pattern. I tried it with my finger first, again just able to make out the rhythm. Then I had my tablet try. This tune was a bit more somber and dignified —a man of business, proud of his position, maybe. The next monument was quicker, almost lilting—a teenager full of life.

I wiped tears away from my eyes. Yes, I was overlaying my own imagery on these simple tunes, and they were *human* images, which couldn't be right. But I was being talked to by a *people* who had been dead a thousand years. And I could hear them.

By this point my fingers had turned bright red and were aching from the cold. I wanted to listen to every one of the thirty-seven monuments, listen to thirty-seven distinct voices, but that would have to wait.

The lander was over a kilometer from the site, but I'm pretty sure I covered the distance in less than five minutes. I spent the next ten hours in my cabin, in front of my computer.

Eventually, though, I had to find Sean to let him know what equipment I was going to need—after swearing him to secrecy. I wasn't sure he even believed what I'd found.

The last thing I did was send an invitation to everyone on the lander, before collapsing into a deep, dreamless sleep.

When I got to the site the next day, Sean had already set up everything I'd asked for, including a tablet to control it all. His beard had kept growing and now, under the plastic breathing mask, it looked like he was actually wearing a breathing mask made of hair. I grinned at him, and he waved back.

Merrick showed up a little while later, along with several members of the other science teams and the ship's crew. In general, crew didn't mix with the science teams, but they were apparently curious. Merrick must have been curious as well, but his expression was blank.

I cleared my throat, suddenly feeling like I was about to give an oral dissertation defense in front of a hostile examination committee. The howling wind was chilling, but I felt sweat trickling down my neck.

"Uh, thank you all for coming. I, uh..."

I seemed to lose all control of my ability to speak. Desperately, I looked around, and saw Sean, standing behind everyone else. He winked at me, and gave me a brief thumbs-up. It helped.

I took a deep breath and started again.

"For the past several weeks, we've been trying to figure out what these stones represent, and whether the markings are writing. I now have a solid working hypothesis."

As if playing for dramatic effect, the wind dropped, leaving us in temporary silence. Most of the faces in front of me were openly interested, perhaps surprised, but Merrick's eyes were narrowed in a look of frustration so intense that I almost took a step backwards. What could possibly be driving that? Was he *that* afraid of being beaten to the finish line?

I took another deep breath, and held my ground.

"Each stone represents something—a concept, or, possibly, individual entities. If so, then this site *is* a graveyard—or at least a *memorial.* But the patterns are not words about each of these people. They are music."

I tapped something on my tablet, and Maggie's tune played out from the speakers Sean had placed around the site. They were highly directional, so the tune came from the location of Maggie's stone. At the same time, a bright light shone on the spiral pattern, travelling in time with the playback.

Everyone turned to look. It was the same melody from yesterday, but my experimentation with the parameters had improved it—added more depth and nuance. I'd heard the tune dozens of times by now, and it still made me shiver. From the looks on the faces of the others, I was not alone.

After a brief explanation of what I'd found, and how the patterns worked, I had the computer play its interpretation of several other stones—the somber business man. The teenager. A playful tune that made me think of an entertainer. A reserved, powerful tune that I associated with a mayor or a captain.

One of the biologists was laughing with glee. Several people were running fingers over the patterns, although with gloves on, it didn't work.

"If we can hear it," said the biologist who'd been laughing, "then that means that the creators had ears as well—heard sounds like we do."

"Not necessarily," said Merrick, and the anger was gone as he sank into the problem. "Sound is just vibrations. They might have had very sensitive fingers—digits—something—that interpreted the vibrations."

"Or antennae or a long sensitive tongue," I added. "There's no way to really know."

Merrick grinned at the image, and just for a second, I grinned back. Then we both looked away.

"Also," I continued, looking directly at the biologist, "the computer has chosen a pentatonic scale for the notes because it seems to fit, and because it sounds reasonable to us—to humans. That's fairly arbitrary, although with more research, we might be able to figure out how it was originally supposed to be interpreted."

The biologist sighed. "It's beautiful," she said," but I still wish you'd found me a body to examine."

There was general laughter at that.

The tune from the last gravestone had faded away, and for a moment I was a little lost, not quite sure how to get back on the track of my presentation. I was rescued by one of the crewmen, a short man in a blue uniform, whose name I couldn't remember.

"What about the big one?" he asked, pointing to the large stone in the center of the graveyard.

I smiled at him. "Glad you asked. That one took a while to figure out. You have to do both spirals at the same time." I hit the icon on my tablet, and a strange rhythmic pulsing started.

The crewman tilted his head to the side, listening. "That doesn't sound like the others. The others sound, well, sound like people. This is more like a back-beat or something..."

I nodded at him, impressed. It had taken me hours to figure that out. "It makes sense when you do *this*."

I hit another icon to run the program I'd spent most of the night on. The computer started up *all* of the monuments, delaying some, letting others fade in and fade out, then repeating them, little glowing lights spiraling throughout the site.

It was like standing in a busy market square, surrounded by people going about their lives. Children running, vendors hawking their wares, officials strutting around, and beneath it all, the *thrum* of the center monument adding life and depth to it all.

I let it run for several minutes, before allowing the individual tunes to fade away.

No one moved or spoke. The only sound was the whistling of the wind. I noticed that the crewman who'd asked the questions had tears in his eyes, and after a moment, I realized that I did, too.

Finally, Sean walked over to me, and gave me a one-armed hug.

"It's beautiful."

I hugged him back, my lip quivering.

"They're going to love this back home," said one of the biologists.

I nodded, and kept my eyes on him, careful not to look towards Merrick. "I sent a report back a few hours ago. I'd normally wait until after we were done, but we only have a few weeks left anyway."

The biologist nodded back in agreement, as though it were the most natural thing in the world to have done. Perhaps I *had* been too cautious in the past.

Out of the corner of my eye I saw Merrick take a step towards me, stop, and then turn and walk away. At least there wasn't going to be a big argument in front of everyone. That was a relief.

Two days later I was sitting at the tiny desk in my cabin when there was a knock at my door. It was Merrick. I tilted my head at him and raised an eyebrow.

"I just wanted to say congratulations."

"Thank you." I kept my voice toneless.

Merrick took a deep breath and stepped into my cabin. He opened his mouth, closed it, then took another deep breath.

"I wanted to let you know that I sent a note to the college, giving you full credit for your previous work on Gliese 837c, and withdrawing my own name."

My eyes widened. "You didn't have to do that."

He shook his head. "I did. The thing is, with all of our conversations, I'd honestly convinced myself that we'd done that work together, and that you were holding me back by refusing to publish. I realize now..."

He swallowed. "I realize now that my contribution was almost nothing. It was all you, just like it was here. I think I need to find another field."

I think my mouth fell open. I thought back over the arguments that I'd had with Merrick. His old words twisted into different shapes in my mind, and I could suddenly see them from his perspective. It was true that most of the Gliese work had been mine, but Merrick *had* contributed quite a bit too. Withdrawing his name would cause a scandal—possibly end his career, or *any* career based on research. I'm not sure that I would have had the courage to do anything like that. I wondered if all of the strange looks he'd been giving me lately had been because he'd been thinking about doing this.

He turned to go, and I watched him disappear down the hallway.

There was something I'd wanted to do ever since I'd realized about the music. It was a definite no-no, and I could get in a lot of trouble...but on the other hand, courage deserved courage.

I found Merrick in his cabin a few days later. He seemed surprised to see me.

"There's something I want to show you," I said.

He shrugged, but stood up.

We picked up our outside gear and cycled out through the airlock. We'd normally turn left to get to the graveyard site, but I turned right and started walking. Merrick seemed slightly surprised, but followed without comment.

We walked on in silence for twenty minutes, while I worked up the courage to speak.

"I've been thinking about what you did," I said, finally. "You were right—it was my research and my ideas, but you helped me flesh them out, and you pushed them into being published. You were right about that too."

Merrick kept his eyes firmly in front of him, his face a mask. I plowed on.

"I've been communicating with the professor. He's agreed to talk to the committee. The report on Gliese 837c is going to be updated to show both of our names—with mine listed first, of course."

Merrick's mouth opened, then closed a few times.

"I...," he started, then stopped. He gave the shortest of nods.

We walked on in silence. I led him to a spot about three kilometers from the ship, four from the graveyard. There was a small section of cliff that you couldn't see unless you were standing in the exact right spot, facing the exact right direction.

Merrick had kept his blank emotionless expression intact since I'd told him about the report, but when he saw the cliff face, he burst out laughing.

"When I said we needed to carve our names in the field, this isn't exactly what I had in mind."

There were three parts to the carving I'd made with Sean's laser rig. At the top was a star chart showing Earth's location, and another chart that showed the current alignment of all of the planets and moons in *this* solar system—on the theory that an advanced culture could use it to calculate precisely when we had been there. Below that were our names—Jenna, Sean and Merrick, etched in our alphabet, and below each of the names was a spiral like on the monuments.

"I figure that if another alien species comes along and finds this site as well as the other, it will drive them completely crazy. I know I shouldn't have done it, but

I had to leave some proof that we'd been here."

Merrick smiled. He tugged off his glove and stepped towards the cliff, then looked back at me for permission. I nodded.

He started with Sean's spiral. As with the graveyard, only the vaguest rhythm was audible. I handed him my tablet, and he pointed it at the pattern and hit play.

Despite loving music, I was no musician, but the computer had helped me. Sean's tune was solid, confident, capable. Merrick nodded before moving on to the other patterns. Mine was inquisitive, changing—a little bit sad. I wasn't quite sure about it, but Sean had sworn that it captured me perfectly.

Merrick's tune was brash and striving, with a deep under-beat—but uplifting, hopeful. When the computer had first played it, I knew that it fit him exactly, although I couldn't have explained precisely why. He played it a second time, running his finger over the pattern as it ran.

When he finally spoke, his voice was so quiet I could barely hear him "Is that how you really see me?"

I nodded.

"Well, then, perhaps I'm not a hopeless case after all."

I smiled. "Don't get ahead of the facts."

See Arlen Feldman's story "Graveyard" online at Metaphorosis.
If you liked it, leave a comment. Authors love that!
Remember to subscribe to our e-mail updates so you'll know when new stories are posted.

About the story

Graveyards always make me wistful. You see an old, pitted grave and you get a name and a date, possibly a quote, and that's about it. Unless it's of someone famous, you'll almost never know anything else about the person—how did they die? How did they live?

There may be a few clues in the graveyard—how expensive the stone, where it is placed in the graveyard, how elaborate...and, more than anything else, the place and the date. 19th century Colorado? 16th century East Anglia? We know about those times, so we can start to make guesses about the person.

But what if the gravestone is on an alien planet with nothing around it? What can you figure out? For one, you know that it was put there by a being trying to memorialize someone or something—assuming it really is a gravestone. Beyond that, what?

That idea was what originally inspired "Graveyard". The idea for the patterns on the stones came from how LPs work, and from a Danish art installation—the Asphaltophone (created by Steen Krarup Jensen and Jakob Freud-Magnus). When you drive over the Asphaltophone, it plays a melody. This idea has since been copied to create a number of "singing roads."

The story didn't really work, though, until I added the two characters who are both worried about how they will leave their mark on the world—which almost certainly also motivated the creators of the graveyard.

A question for the author

Q: Do you write things other than speculative fiction?

A: My background is software, and so my major published works are tome-length books on various topics such as database and user interface programming. Unfortunately, these works are somewhat ephemeral, since the underlying technologies becomes less relevant as time marches on. I only returned to writing fiction after getting out of day-to-day involvement with my company, and most of what I've written and published since then has been speculative fiction, but I have written a few mainstream stories, and a few stories that I really can't quite categorize.

About the author

Arlen Feldman is a software engineer, and co-founder of Cherwell Software, one of the leading service desk products in the world. Now semi-retired, he is also a technical adviser, a slightly published writer of fiction, computer book author, maker, costumer, and a semi-professional dilettante.

cowthulu.com, @ArlenFeldman

Copyright

Metaphorosis Publishing

Metaphorosis offers beautifully written science fiction and fantasy. Our projects include:

Metaphorosis Magazine

Metaphorosis, a weekly magazine of SFF short stories, including stories from all the authors in this anthology. Find out more at magazine.metaphorosis.com, and sign up to be notified of new stories.

Metaphorosis Books

Recent books from Metaphorosis can be found at books.metaphorosis.com, and include:

Metaphorosis 2017

Metaphorosis 2016

All the stories from *Metaphorosis* magazine's second year.

Almost all the stories from *Metaphorosis* magazine's first year.

Metaphorosis: Best of 2017

The best science fiction and fantasy stories from *Metaphorosis'* 2nd year.

Metaphorosis: Best of 2016

The best science fiction and fantasy stories from *Metaphorosis'* 1st year.

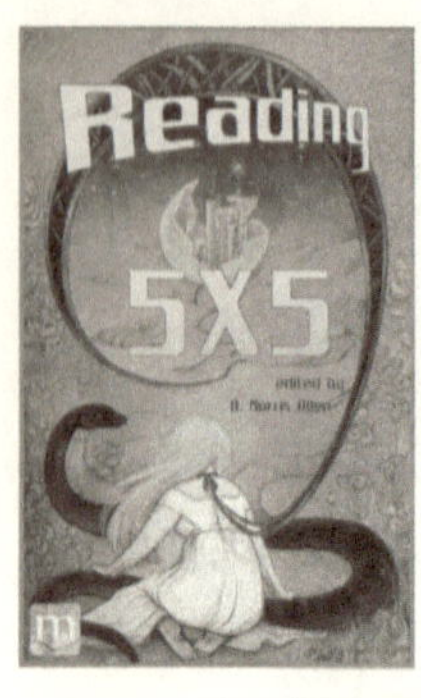

Reading 5X5

Five stories, five times

Twenty-five SFF authors, five base stories, five versions of each – see how different writers take on the same material.

Reading 5X5

Writers' Edition

All the stories from the regular, readers' edition, plus two extra stories, the story seed, and authors' notes.

Best Vegan SFF of 2017

The best vegan science fiction and fantasy stories of 2017!

Best Vegan SFF of 2016

The best vegan science fiction and fantasy stories of 2016!

Susurrus

A darkly romantic story of magic, love, and suffering.

www.ingramcontent.com/pod-product-compliance
Lightning Source LLC
Chambersburg PA
CBHW020527120726
47904CB00003B/985